The flicker of brightness, at ground level, could have been bouncing off a mirror, but the desert

"Run!" Jen shouted. She clapped her heels to Silly's sides and leaned low as the mare surged from a nervous walk into a full gallop.

Sam didn't follow, though her chaotic thoughts finally focused. That crack had been a rifle shot. There was no way she'd leave the Phantom here alone, to face a gunman.

But a man with a rifle wasn't a mustang's natural enemy. The Phantom shouldn't charge; he should run.

The rest of his herd fled, but the Phantom rushed away from his family, toward the sound. His flint-hard hooves made every step count. He was homing in on the enemy.

Should she go after him? Sam tried to think. She might keep the horse from being shot, but if a stray bullet struck her, she'd be no good to him.

Read all the books about the

Phantom Stallion

Phantom Stallion

∞ 11 ∞
Untamed

TERRI FARLEY

AVON BOOKS

An Imprint of HarperCollins*Publishers*

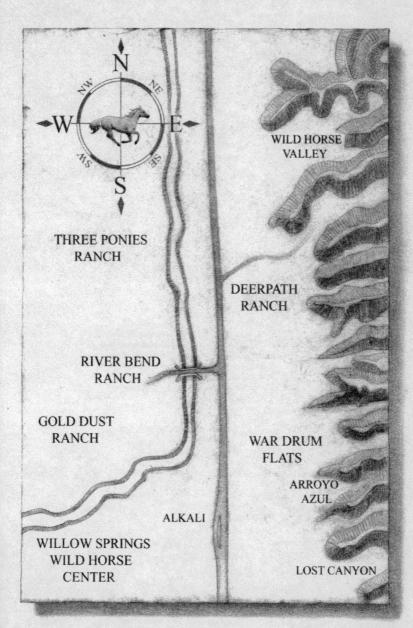

Chapter One ❧

Samantha Forster had made a huge discovery at school. It wasn't a good discovery, but it might benefit humankind to know a girl couldn't die from embarrassment. Otherwise, she'd be dead.

As Sam trudged into the kitchen at River Bend Ranch, she heard the vacuum cleaner sucking at the rugs in the rooms upstairs. Outside, only the horses had greeted her. Dad and the cowboys were out on the range. Her stepmother Brynna was at work, and Gram was vacuuming upstairs.

For a while, she was alone with her humiliation, and she was glad.

Sam slumped into a chair. She closed her eyes. Next, she buried her face in her hands. Nothing helped. She could see the scene in Journalism class as if it were still happening.

Mr. Blair, her Journalism teacher, had ordered everyone who wanted to be an editor next year to apply for the position. Sam had sort of wanted to be photo editor and Rjay, the editor in chief, had urged her to apply. So she'd filled out the form. But that wasn't enough for Mr. Blair.

He'd insisted applicants explain to the class, aloud, why they should get the jobs.

Today, when Sam had gasped at the announcement, someone nearby had whispered, "It's not like he didn't *tell* us."

Sam hadn't turned to see who it was, because the British lilt in that voice meant it could only belong to Rachel Slocum. Wealthy, conceited, and unfairly pretty, Rachel loved seeing Sam suffer.

Sam tried not to give her that pleasure.

Besides, it wasn't like she was afraid to give a talk. Just a couple of weeks ago, Sam had overcome her fear of public speaking to make a presentation to the student council. This should be even easier. At least that's what she told herself.

True, she wasn't prepared, but all she had to do was think of three main points. It had worked before.

Easier still, she could just listen to what everyone else said, and do something similar.

Then Mr. Blair had called on her first.

Quickly, she'd flipped her fingers through her

auburn hair, and straightened her shoulders inside her teal-blue sweater.

She glimpsed Rjay giving her a thumbs-up signal across the room as she began.

"I want to be photo editor because I'm a visual person, a hard worker, and . . ." She'd taken a deep breath and pictured herself at a football game on a gray, sleety afternoon. "And I don't mind being kept outside."

Kept outside? She'd bitten her lip.

"With the horses?" Rachel Slocum pretended to be confused.

Sam glared at her, but Rachel didn't notice. Dressed in a champagne-colored jumpsuit made of raw silk, Rachel should have looked like she was draped in a parachute. She didn't.

Head tossed back with her furry, mink-brown eyelashes half lowered, Rachel was soaking up the appreciative giggles of the rest of the class.

Eager to explain, Sam had blurted, "What I mean—is that I don't mind after-school photo shoes."

That mistake had turned the giggles to outright laughter.

"Photo *shoots*," she'd said, raising her voice, nearly shouting, but by then even Mr. Blair and Rjay were chuckling. "Obviously, I'm better with pictures than words."

Wasn't that just a little bit funny? Apparently not, because the laughter dwindled. As it did, Sam saw

Rjay pointing forcefully at a clipping tacked to the class bulletin board.

Got it.

Rjay's support had helped erase a bit of her embarrassment. She'd smiled and opened her mouth to remind her classmates she'd not only had a photograph published in a real newspaper, but she'd won second prize in the Night Magic contest.

But before she pronounced a syllable, Rachel spoke up again.

"Quit laughing. She *was* kicked in the head by a horse, you know." Rachel's words had oozed with false sympathy and the entire room had gone silent.

"Not funny, Slocum," Mr. Blair snapped. "Let's go on to the next applicant."

"That would be me," Rachel said, smoothly. She walked to the front of the classroom instead of speaking from her seat. "I'm sure someone is bound to point out that I'm not an experienced photographer." Rachel tilted her head Sam's way. "But working with advertising, I've developed a sense for how things look on the page.

"More importantly, I've got big plans for dispensing with that old-fashioned photo lab . . ." Rachel gestured toward the class darkroom.

Sam's spirits had fallen even more. The darkroom was old-fashioned, but it was a great place to escape for secret conversations.

"Next year, we're going all digital," Rachel said,

as if she'd already won the position. "The school newspapers winning national prizes work that way and so should we."

"We can't afford digital cameras," RJay reminded her.

But Sam had known what was coming and her eyes had darted briefly to Mr. Blair's. His expression said he, too, knew how Rachel would answer.

"I'm sure something will turn up," Rachel assured the class, then strode confidently back to her desk.

Mr. Blair had called up other students, one by one, but Sam hadn't really heard any of them. She could stand competing with Rachel. She could stand messing up in front of the class, too. Neither of those things was half as bad as all the faces that had turned the other way when she caught them staring.

Running against Rachel's money and an accusation of brain damage, how could she possibly win?

Sam glanced at the kitchen clock at the same time the vacuum cleaner sighed to silence upstairs. She only had forty-five minutes before she was supposed to meet Jen for their ride.

She hadn't told Jen about the episode in Journalism and she didn't want to tell Gram.

Gram was almost psychic when it came to Sam. If they spent five minutes together in this kitchen, she'd weasel the whole story out of her.

Sam shot to her feet, moving so quickly she accidentally stepped on Cougar's tail.

The brown-striped cat squalled.

"I'm sorry, kitty," Sam apologized, but Cougar darted out of the kitchen.

Once your day started downhill, it was hard to push it back up. But Sam was determined to send it in a better direction.

She and her best friend Jennifer Kenworthy had talked all the way home on the hot, stuffy bus about riding out to Aspen Creek. There, they hoped to see a young black mustang she'd named New Moon.

Moon was the Phantom's son and last year, before winter set in, he'd managed to steal one red bay mare from his father's herd. There was no guarantee he still had the mare or that warmer weather had brought him back to the aspen grove, but they were willing to take a chance.

One thing could improve my luck, Sam thought.

She felt silly and superstitious letting the possibility cross her mind, but what if she could find the braided horsehair bracelet she'd woven from strands of the Phantom's mane?

Not that it was magical. Not really. Somehow, though, it always improved her understanding of horses, especially wild ones.

The bracelet had been lost for months. And the way things were going, it wasn't likely to resurface today.

Sam was halfway up the stairs to her bedroom when the tension that had gripped her since Journalism suddenly relaxed its hold.

"I know where it is," Sam muttered in amazement.

The revelation was like falling through a trapdoor. She'd hidden the bracelet. She knew exactly where it was.

Sam skipped over the last two stairs and nearly collided with her grandmother.

"Hello, dear," Gram said, tucking a strand of gray hair back into the red bandanna tied over her head. "I didn't hear you come in."

Sam kissed Gram's cheek.

"You must be having a good day," Gram said, chuckling.

"Getting better every minute," Sam said, and she meant it.

Cougar had taken refuge from her tail-tromping clumsiness in a sunbeam that was warming the patchwork star on her white quilt. He kept his eyes determinedly closed as Sam moved a stack of books balanced atop her dresser and dropped them onto the floor.

The books had served as a barricade in front of a dusty tin box.

"I found it!"

Her shout was too much, and the cat jumped down from his napping place.

"I don't feel a bit sorry for you," Sam said as Cougar gave an insulted hiss and ran for the door. "It's your fault it was lost."

From the first day her friend Jake Ely had given her Cougar, the cat had been curious and energetic. When he'd spotted the bracelet on her wrist, he'd pounced.

She'd tried to turn the kitten's attention to dangling yarn and Ping-Pong balls, but he refused to be distracted.

Gently, she'd tried to discourage him, by setting him in another room. Every time, Cougar had leaped for her wrist, batting and scratching, treating the bracelet like a live creature.

Finally, she'd decided the bracelet was too precious to be a cat toy.

Sam lifted the tin box and blew the dust from its top.

The hiding place she'd chosen was a button box that had once been her mom's. The round tin was a tarnished gold color.

Sam pried the lid off and set it aside. There, atop hundreds of multicolored buttons, sat the bracelet. She slipped it over her wrist.

It had been right here in her bedroom, all along.

Sam held her arm high. Late afternoon sunlight turned the scratchy circlet the same silver as the Phantom. It was hard to believe the wild stallion had actually allowed her to run her fingers through his mane.

Before she pressed the button box lid back into place, Sam let her fingertips trace its raised black-

and-gold pattern. The decoration showed a running black horse. He pulled a sleigh carrying a man and a woman. A child sat snuggled between them.

Sam sighed. She'd been almost five when her mother died. Now she was almost fourteen.

"And I'm over it," Sam said aloud.

Still, she kept the button box on her lap a few minutes more. She shook the tin—Gram said it had once held a Christmas fruitcake—and watched the buttons shift around.

There were a few wooden spools of thread and stray sewing needles inside, along with hundreds of buttons in shades of brown, black, gray, green, white, and blue.

Sam spotted a tiny yellow button painted with violets. She'd bet it was from some outfit she'd worn as a baby.

She smiled at the idea of the bracelet hiding inside her mother's button box.

"Thanks, Mom," she said, then slapped her hand over her mouth.

That's crazy, Sam thought.

She couldn't believe she'd said it. She held her breath, listening for footsteps. What if Gram had heard her?

As the thought popped into her mind, she heard the phone ring and Gram answer it.

Sam took a deep breath. She should get downstairs and have a snack if she planned to have one. She had to get moving if she was going to meet Jen on time.

There were a lot of things she should be doing, but she couldn't pry her fingers from this box that her mother had touched.

And then she knew why. Something pink and out of place was nestled among the sewing supplies.

Sam shook the box, then fished out a scrap of crumpled pink paper. It looked like stationery, folded into a small square.

Slowly, Sam unfolded it. It wasn't a letter, but a list.

Sam sucked in a breath. Her heartbeat echoed in her wrists and temples. The handwriting was her mother's.

Something like magnetism drew her eyes past the items on the list. Five words stood alone at the bottom edge of the paper.

There Sam read, in her mother's firm, scrolling handwriting, *No harm to the horses.*

Chapter Two ✑

"Samantha!" Gram's exasperated tone said this wasn't the first time she'd called up the stairs.

Sam actually had to turn her head to force her eyes away from her mother's words.

"Yes?" Sam couldn't put the pink paper back inside, but she pressed the lid back on the button box and stood up.

"Jen called to say she was leaving her house," Gram said. "If you're riding to meet her, you'd better hurry."

"I'm coming," Sam said. Her hands trembled as she stared at her mom's handwriting.

She shouldn't take the time to read this now. But how could she stop? This list offered her what she hadn't had in eight years: a few moments with her mother.

Besides, that last line had the ring of a vow.

No harm to the horses.

Which horses? River Bend's? A band of wild mustangs? What had Mom meant? Had she lived long enough to protect the horses she obviously loved?

Although Sam's eyes lingered on the words, she knew she had to look away. The rest of the list might help her understand what her mother had meant.

She skimmed it once, quickly.

Was it a shopping list? A to-do list?

Sam read it carefully.

· *Grace m.d. (cool apron?)*
· *Sam try on summer clothes (new shorts/ sunsuits?)*
· *Antelope season/Crossing/horses??? check w/NDW? BLM? Bow/rifle?*
· *Wh forage*
· *Caleb crim record ????*
· *Darton Deli: ham, Swiss ch, past, lasag. stuff, aspirin and chili rub for Dally*
· *No harm to the horses*

Her mother's note was riddled with personal abbreviations. Not all of them made sense to Sam, but there was no mistaking that last one.

The note was too important to rush and too

precious to leave behind.

Carefully, Sam folded it into a neat square, then eased it into the front pocket of her jeans.

She hurried down the stairs, grabbed the brownie Gram offered, then jogged toward the barn.

The saddle horses in the ten-acre corral lifted their heads from grazing to watch her. Buddy, her nearly yearling heifer, ambled up to the fence chewing. Ace, Sam's pretty bay mustang, neighed in three short bursts.

"Coming, Ace," she told her horse, but she didn't stop to reassure him or to rub Buddy's head. It would be faster to just grab her tack and hurry back.

After weeks of reconstruction following a scary earthquake, the barn still smelled like freshly sawed lumber. Sam grabbed her saddle and bridle from the tack room and hefted them against the front of her, trying to balance and walk fast at the same time.

She'd almost reached the pasture when Jeepers-Creepers trotted across the wooden bridge, with Dad astride.

"You thinkin' about doin' any chores before you go out to play?" Dad called.

With a jean jacket pulled over his shirt and his Christmas-new gray Stetson, Dad looked like every kid's mental picture of a cowboy.

"When I get back," Sam shouted, as she led Ace from the pasture and began saddling him.

As Dad rode closer and she saw the smile white

against his darkly tanned face, Sam decided Dad wasn't serious about making her work. She released a breath she hadn't known she was holding.

Thinking of the note in her pocket, Sam tried to look at Dad as if she weren't his daughter.

Dad had been a college student when he'd fallen in love with Mom. How had he looked on the day he'd proposed? And on the day Mom had died?

Sam shook her head as if she could dispel the awful image.

One thing was sure: he hadn't been the thin, dusty man he was today. And his heart had belonged to her mother, Louise, not to her *step*mother, Brynna.

Sam tightened her saddle cinch and tucked in the loose end. She slid her hand between the cinch and Ace's warm belly.

Dad drew rein next to her. Warmth radiated from Jeepers, River Bend's only Appaloosa. He stamped and blew through his lips, glad to be home.

She should show Dad the note. He'd decipher her mother's abbreviations, and remember what had motivated Mom to write *No harm to the horses.*

She *would* show him. Absolutely.

But not now.

"Brynna's bringing Penny when she comes home from work. I know you wanted to be here," Dad said.

Sam glanced up at the faint appeal in Dad's voice, then unhooked her stirrup from her saddle horn and let it flop down.

Dad knew her relationship with Brynna was uneasy: comfortable one day, edgy the next.

Brynna was the director of the Willow Springs Wild Horse Center, where hundreds of mustangs brought in from the range lived until they were adopted.

She cared more for wild horses than anyone else Sam knew. And, maybe because she was younger than Dad, Brynna allowed Sam to do a lot of things Dad questioned.

Sam knew Brynna was probably the best stepmother she could have hoped for, if she'd hoped for one. But she hadn't.

How would Brynna feel about this note?

Sam's stomach gave a nervous lurch. She didn't want to know. She'd guess that in spite of the last line about the horses, Brynna would be hurt. That part about buying ingredients for lasagna, for instance, might make her worry. Brynna wasn't much of a cook.

"We'll need to be extra watchful," Dad said, snagging Sam's mind back. "Penny bein' blind and all."

"Yeah," Sam answered. She'd nearly forgotten Brynna's mustang mare had lost her sight during her failed adoption.

The arrival of a new horse would be exciting, but since the saddle herd didn't always welcome newcomers, they'd put Penny in a pipe corral next to the ten-acre pasture so the horses could get used to each other.

When Ace had been the low horse in the pasture, he hadn't been so lucky. He'd suffered lots of bites and kicks. The others had only accepted him a few weeks ago. Sam was convinced it was because the little gelding had gained new self-confidence while she was training him for the Superbowl of Horsemanship.

They'd need to watch over the blind mare. Dad was right about that. But first, she had to meet Jen.

"I won't be long," Sam said as she swung into the saddle.

Dad looked skeptical, but he let her leave.

With Sam in the saddle, Ace tossed his head in a figure-eight movement, eager to be off. A restful winter and the Superbowl of Horsemanship cross-country race two weeks ago had combined to put Ace in high spirits. He'd bolt into a run if she'd let him. Instead, Sam eased him into a jog.

When the gelding arched his neck and obeyed, Sam's mind veered back to the note.

Brynna and Dad had met last summer when Dad had driven Sam up to see Willow Springs for the first time.

Even though Dad was a third-generation cattle-man and not a fan of the Bureau of Land Management, a spark had jumped between him and Brynna right away.

Sam had overheard Brynna telling Gram that it had taken one single minute for them to know they were meant for each other, but one hundred days to decide to marry.

After crossing the bridge, Sam reined Ace right. She noticed a fuzz of low grass and weeds spreading out from their usual dirt trail.

Suddenly, a fragment from her mother's note made sense.

Sam tightened her reins. Ace snorted. His gait turned choppy.

"Oh, come on, whoa," she told him.

Ace halted, but kept tossing his head, letting her know he was aggravated by the stop.

Sam rose in her stirrups, took the note from her pocket, and looked at it again.

3. Antelope season/Crossing/horses???

There were the horses, again, but what did it mean?

Antelope Crossing was a flat plain covered with sagebrush and bunch grass and it wasn't far away. But is that what Mom had meant? Or had she meant Antelope *hunting* season? Maybe Mom had capitalized Crossing accidentally.

Maybe, Sam thought, swallowing hard, she'd only thought of Antelope Crossing because it was where her mother had died.

She sat quietly, holding her reins in her left hand while she turned her horsehair bracelet with her right.

Mom had been killed while driving her VW bus. She'd swerved to miss a herd of antelope. The bus had run off the road and rolled.

She'd been killed instantly.

That's what everyone said.

But Mom's note hinted that something had been going on out there.

Ace tensed beneath her. The little bay mustang had picked up on her anxiety.

"Nothing to worry about," Sam said, leaning forward to rub his neck. "But it might be worth a look."

Sam loosened her reins, leaned forward, and sent Ace into a lope. Antelope Crossing was just beyond the aspen grove where they'd been planning to ride anyway.

She stared at the range ahead and saw a rider outlined against a blue sky marked with windblown clouds called mare's tails.

In seconds, she realized it was Jen and Silk Stockings, her high-strung palomino.

Perfect, Sam thought. Jen had come well past halfway to meet her, so they had more time. If she told Jen about the note, she knew her friend would go with her.

Jen wore a green quilted vest over a yellow ribbed sweater and her white-blond braids were bound with yellow yarn. With the back of her hand, she gave her glasses a push back up her nose.

"What's up?" Jen said. Sam watched in admiration as Jen slowed the palomino to a walk, then stopped her within two feet of Ace. "You look kind of freaked out."

"I don't know," Sam began. "I just . . . I think . . ."

"You must know." Jen used her usual logic to evaluate Sam's discomfort. "Or you wouldn't be fumbling for words."

"You're right, but I still don't know what to say. Here." Sam pulled the note from her pocket and held it out to Jen.

"Is this something bad?" Jen asked before she took it. Sam lifted her shoulders so high, they brushed her hair. "Not exactly."

Hesitantly, Jen took the pink paper and unfolded it. While she read, Silly extended her golden nose to Ace's bay one, then looked around, ears swiveling to take in the faraway rush of the La Charla River.

Sam watched Jen until she looked up, frowning. "It's from my mom," she said.

"I figured that out," Jen said with a lopsided smile. "The part about you trying on sunsuits tipped me off."

Sam nodded. This was what she adored about her best friend. Jen could smile about something sad, and make it seem exactly the right thing to do.

"How does it make you feel?" Jen asked.

"Kind of like I'm excited and scared at the same time."

"Because she wrote it right before she died," Jen said. It wasn't a question.

"Why do you say that?" Sam yelped, while Jen nodded in understanding. "What makes you think she wrote it just . . . before?"

"Logic," Jen said, handing the note back to Sam. "She mentions a Mother's Day present for your Gram, and the antelope." Jen lowered her voice to a near whisper. "And she died the Saturday before Mother's Day, trying not to hit those antelope."

Sam stared at the note. *1. Grace m.d. (cool apron?).*

Jen was right! "m.d." meant Mother's Day, and her mom had been thinking about buying Gram an apron. How could she have missed that?

"You're brilliant," Sam congratulated Jen.

"Not really. You would've figured it out," Jen assured her.

"So will you ride out to Antelope Crossing with me? Now?"

"Are you joking?" Jen said, "Of course I'll go. It's like she left you a message."

Sam took a deep breath. She'd hoped for Jen's cooperation, but Jen was even more intrigued than she would have guessed.

"There's nothing mystical about it," Sam insisted.

"I didn't say there was." Jen gave a sigh, then tipped her head to one side, peering through her glasses with an owlish expression. "But this note sounds like a warning. Like something bad was going on out there, something putting the horses in danger."

Chills skittered down Sam's arms and legs.

"I know," she said, slowly. "And even though it may be too late, it's up to me to discover what it was."

Chapter Three ❧

"We'd better get going," Jen said, glancing toward the sun. Its brightness shone from behind the mountains now, signaling evening was on its way.

Sam swung Ace alongside Silly, and the two horses settled into a side-by-side gallop across the range. Black mane and white, brown legs and golden, showed that the two horses were as different as their riders, but just as well suited to each other.

Without speaking, Sam and Jen agreed to ride past the bridge that led to River Bend Ranch. Even though there was a more direct trail that climbed the ridge overlooking the Forsters' two-story white house, they didn't take it. If they cut through River Bend, Dad or Gram would call them back to shovel out stalls or something.

Instead, they cut left on a rougher trail that ran along the border between River Bend and the Elys' Three Ponies Ranch.

After navigating the terrain between the two ranches, they crested the ridge, then took the downhill trail to Aspen Creek.

"No sign of Moon," Sam said, glancing around.

Although the young black stallion had been here in the late fall, the place looked completely different now.

Tender green leaves had replaced the aspen trees' crisp golden ones. The footing was still damp, not with mud as before, but with shallow pools of melted snow. Each pool held green islands that were really beach ball–sized tufts of grass.

The horses slowed as they splashed through the cold water, and Sam finally asked, "How did you know about my mom?"

Jen sighed. "My mom talks about the accident every Mother's Day, and each time we see a herd of pronghorn. She liked your mother a lot. They went riding together, and out to movies." Jen looked at Sam, probably thinking they did the same things. "She always says your mom's death was senseless."

"I'd like to talk with your mom, about mine," Sam said.

"No problem," Jen said, but her tone was distracted and she frowned at the trees surrounding them.

Sam knew why Jen looked uneasy. The last time they'd been here, cougars had been on the prowl. But they were gone now, and Sam had bigger things to worry over.

"Right after it happened, I couldn't ask my dad to tell me much," Sam explained.

"Well, you were only five years old."

"Yeah, but that's not why. Every time I asked, it made him sad. How do you think a little kid feels, making her father cry?"

Jen shook her head, but then her melancholy look dropped away. "I bet he could talk about it now. They say it helps keep a person's memory alive to talk about them."

"You're probably right," Sam said.

As the earth beneath the horses' hooves grew dry, they rode more quickly. It was warmer, now that they were out of the shaded Aspen Creek Canyon.

"Snake Head Peak," Jen said, pointing to a rock formation jutting from the nearby hills.

"Creepy name," Sam said. The gray granite ahead wore a spiky halo of sun. "Does anyone live over there?"

"Yeah, a guy who's sort of a hermit."

Sam cleared her throat. "Look how nice Mrs. Allen turned out to be," she said. "And I thought she was a hermit."

"Yeah," Jen said. She didn't sound convinced.

The first thing Sam noticed as they came to the

edge of a wide plain was the shadow. Snake Head Peak cast a column of darkness over the sagebrush and bunch grass-covered flat.

Sam had just decided they were on a wild goose chase when something moved. Suddenly, she wasn't looking at a monochrome landscape.

A herd of grazing mustangs and pronghorn covered the flat.

Ace and Silly snorted and danced, but the wild animals had long since picked up the scent of the intruders.

Antelope and wild horses.

Sam's hand fell from the reins, about to touch her mother's note. Ace was too spooked already to risk rustling paper where he couldn't see it. Besides, she didn't need to look. She knew what the note said. Her pulse pounded and her eyes swept the plain, looking for danger.

The brown and white antelope had black horns that seemed perfectly aligned with their dark eyes. They were small, maybe three feet tall, and they'd frozen statue still among the horses.

There. As two blood bay mares showed themselves amid the mustang herd, Sam's heart bounded up with joy. Those two ran with the Phantom's band. She couldn't see him, but the great silver stallion had to be nearby.

Ace bolted forward, reminding Sam that this had once been his herd. She tightened her reins and Ace stopped, but his tail moved in a resentful swish.

Some silent signal flashed among the pronghorn. Like multicolored popcorn, they bounded, not up, but in long leaps, from a dozen spots within the herd of mustangs.

Sam couldn't catch enough breath to speak to Jen.

The pronghorn were coming this way. Slender and graceful as deer, they turned so she could see the cinnamon swatches on their backs. Their cheeks and chests were milky white.

Once separated from the mustang herd, they joined together. *For safety*, Sam thought. Their leaps were amazingly broad and they'd moved so close that Sam could see some had faces marked with black bands.

Then they turned.

Like a flock of birds, they moved as one until she could only see their white rumps fleeing across the range, away from the horses.

"I can't believe . . ." Sam began.

She was thinking of Mom and the notes she'd left behind. Something about the antelope and mustangs had worried her mother, but Sam only saw their beauty.

A flash of silver caught Sam's attention. Ace bunched beneath her and then she heard a stallion's scream.

The Phantom rushed through his mares, scattering them as he galloped.

Sam had seen this charge before. She searched for an intruding stallion.

"There," Jen said, pointing.

Sam saw the clump of sagebrush, but no horse.

"What are you—?"

The flicker of brightness, at ground level, could have been a match, or light bouncing off a mirror, but then a crack of lightning rolled through the desert air.

"Run!" Jen shouted. She clapped her heels to Silly's sides and leaned low as the mare surged from a nervous walk into a full gallop. Jen's white-blond braids mixed with the palomino's flaxen mane.

Sam didn't follow, though her chaotic thoughts finally focused. That crack had been a rifle shot. There was no way she'd leave the Phantom here alone, to face a gunman.

But a man with a rifle wasn't a mustang's natural enemy. The Phantom shouldn't charge; he should run.

The rest of his herd fled as a big honey-brown mare led them after the antelope. Far out on the plain, they were nothing more than bouncing dots, but the horses followed.

The Phantom rushed away from his family, toward the sound.

Muscular and gleaming, he flowed like liquid silver around sagebrush and rocks. His flint-hard hooves made every step count. He was homing in on the enemy.

Once, the Phantom had been tame. He might have been tolerant of men, if they hadn't penned him, strangled him with ropes, pursued and nearly poisoned him.

Captivity had taught him not to fear men.

Freedom had taught him to hate them.

Should she go after him? Sam tried to think. She might keep the horse from being shot, but if a stray bullet struck her, she'd be no good to him.

Chapter Four ❧

"**S**top!" Sam shouted.

Ace shied violently. His head swung left and his black mane flared. His hooves stuttered, trying to reverse direction. Sam settled deeper in her saddle and even though Ace took it as a signal to move forward, she only lost a stirrup in working to control him.

"Hey, boy, you're okay," she crooned to Ace, past teeth threatening to chatter.

Sure, there's just someone shooting at us.

Sam tightened her grip on the reins. It wouldn't do Ace or the Phantom any good for her to panic. Her brain knew that, but every instinct clamored for her to get out of here. Now!

Ace shook his head against the snugged reins and made a low complaint. Sam glanced over her shoulder in time to see the shadowy figure bend.

By the time Ace turned as she'd asked him to do, the man was scuttling away.

"After him," Sam whispered, but she kept Ace at a jog as she rode after the gunman.

She must get a good look at him if she hoped to describe him to Dad, Brynna, and Sheriff Ballard. But the clump of sagebrush was too far away—at least the length of a football field—and Snake Head Peak shaded the man so that even his outline was indistinct.

And then the shooter vanished. No matter how Sam widened her eyes or squinted, she saw nothing.

A passing wind sounded like an eerie intake of breath.

There was no man and no movement. For one stomach-turning instant, Sam remembered what Rachel had said.

She was kicked in the head by a horse, you know.

What if something *was* wrong with her? Sam didn't want to think about it, but it was possible. The shock of Blackie's hoof had knocked her unconscious. She'd been hospitalized for weeks. Then she'd had to live in San Francisco so that a relapse didn't strike when she was far from medical care.

What if her brain was damaged and it had taken the content of Mom's note and scrambled it into a sick fantasy?

No. Jen had definitely heard the shot—and galloped off.

The Phantom had been after something, but now even he seemed confused. He slowed to a hammering trot, then halted. Head high, tendons taut, he stood like a sculpture of equine power.

Sam didn't stop when the stallion did.

The Phantom might be satisfied that danger was gone, but she wasn't. The man could be hiding.

She clenched her molars together. Even if he'd vanished, a man with a gun would have left evidence behind and she'd find it.

Slowly, the stallion's head turned in Sam's direction and all her distress vanished.

His Arab ears pricked forward. His muzzle jerked skyward before he greeted her with a low nicker.

Then the stallion's foreleg struck out. The muscles in his shoulder stretched and bunched. He looked entirely wild as he rose into a half rear. He shook his head so vigorously, his mane blurred as it rayed around him.

As his front hooves touched down, a faraway neigh summoned him. Sam turned with the stallion, hearing his family calling.

The Phantom bobbed his head once more, then wheeled and bolted away. Only the herbal smell of crushed sagebrush remained.

Sam didn't have long to savor her awe.

"You are a nutcase, Samantha Forster!" Jen yelled from about twenty feet away. She leaned sideways in her saddle, as if her voice would carry better aimed around Silly's head.

"And if you think I'm coming within range of a maniac with a rifle to get you, you're a lunatic, too!"

Jen's palomino tossed her forelock back to watch Ace. She sidestepped, sniffed, and the furrows over her dark eyes were easy to recognize as worry.

"He's gone," Sam shouted back, pretending bravery she didn't have. "I'm just going over to where he was, and see what kind of clues he left."

Jen's jaw actually dropped in astonishment. Sam would have laughed if her friend's expression hadn't instantly changed to fury.

"Oh no, you're not."

With the quick skill that marked her horsemanship, Jen sent Silly into Ace's path, blocking Sam.

In response, Ace hunkered down in his cutting horse stance. He'd interpreted Silly's move as a challenge.

"*You* knock it off, too," Jen said, shaking her finger at the little bay mustang.

Ace planted each hoof in stubbornness. He looked away from Jen, but kept one ear tipped in her direction.

Sam rubbed Ace's neck, but it was Jen she needed to convince. "Jen, the guy is gone. He is."

Her words hung there until Jen said, "Maybe it

wasn't a 'he.' Maybe it was . . . something else."

"You heard the gunshot, didn't you?" Sam asked.

With precise thoughtfulness, Jen lifted each braid back over her shoulders. "I heard something."

Sam bit her lip. Jen prided herself on acting cool and level-headed, so Sam didn't remind her that she was the one who'd shouted that they should run.

"It was a shot, all right. He took one from behind that sagebrush," Sam said, pointing. "And that's when you spotted him. But after you took off, I saw him stand up and take aim."

"And that's when you started yelling," Jen concluded.

"I said 'no!'" Sam admitted.

"You quite definitely yelled," Jen corrected her.

"Whatever," Sam said.

"So, if someone's really shooting at wild horses, he's breaking the law, and we should call the sheriff. Are you willing to call Sheriff Ballard?"

"Of course! Why wouldn't I be?"

Jen gave an uncomfortable shrug and looked past Sam.

"Jen, why shouldn't we?" Sam repeated.

"No reason," Jen sighed. "So let's go see what's over there."

Ace and Silly read their riders' calm and fell into a walk.

If only Jake were here, Sam thought. Her friend Jake Ely was an incredible tracker. Sam smiled. If

Jake were tracking this guy, he'd not only follow him, he'd be able to tell where the guy bought his boots and probably what he'd had for breakfast.

But Jake wasn't here, so Sam tried to remember the tips he'd given her before, like using the angle of the sun to highlight the tracks. Above all, she knew to be careful where she walked.

"Probably," Jen said, as if she were reading Sam's mind, "we should get off the horses, so we don't destroy any evidence."

"Probably," Sam agreed, but then she scanned the nearby terrain. The shadow of Snake Head Peak mixed with the gloom of twilight. "But I don't know where that guy went."

"Sam, the odds are, he just likes to hunt," Jen said, sensibly. "He was probably trying to poach a pronghorn, not kill a wild horse or—your hands are shaking."

"No they're not," she said, but her bravery was leaking away and nothing remained but weakness.

The horses had taken another dozen steps when Sam realized what Jen had said.

"Poaching?" Sam asked, then. "What does that mean, exactly?"

"The department of wildlife, or some government bureau, sets up certain seasons when people can hunt animals. I can't believe that it's all right to hunt pronghorn when it's time for their fawns to be born."

Sam felt everything go still.

"My mom's note mentioned antelope season," she said.

"Just stop," Jen said, impatiently. "For one thing, pronghorn aren't technically antelope, though some people use *pronghorn* and *antelope* interchangeably."

"Yes, but—"

"The note also mentioned ham and Swiss cheese, so let's not overreact to what your mom wrote."

Jen's sympathy had apparently come to an end.

Maybe she was right, but Sam still felt as if there were too many coincidences. She stayed in the saddle, ready to make a quick getaway.

Jen dismounted, ground-tied Silly, then peered over the clump of sagebrush, hands on hips.

"Well, someone was here," Jen said. "Look at that."

Curiosity pushed aside fear. Sam scrambled down from Ace and stood beside Jen.

She didn't need the fading sun to see the piece of brass or the clear imprint of a reclining human form.

"Look," Sam said, pointing at two little dents in the sand. "You can see where he propped himself up on his elbows, just waiting."

Sam wiggled her fingers into her pockets.

"What are you doing?" Jen asked. "I'm not going to look at your list again."

"Killing a wild horse is a felony. I'm looking for something to wrap that bullet thing in, for evidence."

"It's a shell casing. The bullet explodes out, and

leaves that behind when you shoot," Jen said.

"Shell casing," Sam repeated. The words sounded official, like she'd discovered real evidence.

"I might have something in my saddlebags," Jen said. "What do you—?"

"A plastic sandwich bag would be perfect. That's what they use on television to preserve the finger-prints and stuff. They can do a DNA test, and—"

"Sam, will you listen to yourself?" Jen said, pulling exactly what they needed from her saddlebags.

She tipped the bag upside down, shook out a few crumbs, blew in it, then shook it again, as if she were killing time.

As she handed the baggie to Sam, Jen took a deep breath. Her voice had softened by the time she went on.

"I know that note was sort of a shock, but it wasn't, well, a warning from beyond the grave. You know that, right?"

Sam felt as if Jen had slapped her. She shook off the surprise, though, realizing why Jen was so skep-tical. This coincidence was just too neat. Finding the note, then seeing the pronghorn and horses and the gunman. But coincidences did happen. That's why there was a name for them!

She was filled with a rare sort of energy as she tried to explain.

"Here's what I know," she told Jen. "My mom's note mentioned antelope and wild horses, and here they were, right where she said to look for them. The note mentioned antelope season and a rifle, and what do we see? A guy shooting during the wrong time of year."

"Probably," Jen said. "I don't know that for sure."

"You're right," Sam said with conviction. "And I think since my mom mentioned a guy named Caleb, with a criminal record, that was probably him."

"Sam," Jen's voice soared. "There were like a dozen question marks after that part of the list!"

"Four," Sam corrected. She'd practically memorized the list already. "There were only four question marks. And if he does have a criminal record, that shell casing could put him in jail."

"For trying to *harm the horses*," Jen finished patiently. "And that's not a crazy thing to say."

She was glad Jen agreed, but why had she put it that way?

Sam used the baggie to pick up the little brass tube, then jiggled it until it fell inside.

Now Jen was chattering about going to Crane Crossing Mall to get new jeans. So everything was all right.

Sam told herself not to be paranoid.

Jen wasn't in Journalism class, so she couldn't have heard what Rachel had said.

Even in a small town like Darton, gossip didn't travel that fast. Did it?

Chapter Five ❧

Copper chestnut and fine-boned as a Thorough-bred, Penny took careful backward steps out of the horse trailer.

Riding toward home, Sam had seen Brynna towing the horse trailer, and followed it across the bridge and into the ranch yard.

Brynna was easing her adopted mustang from the trailer while Gram, Dad, and the cowboys watched.

Glossy and alert, Penny sniffed and listened. She searched out the details of her new home like any sighted horse.

"She's beautiful, Brynna." Sam said with a sigh.

And she was. About fourteen and a half hands high, the mare had two low white socks that looked as if she'd dipped her front hooves in sugar. Her legs and body were slim and she tilted her head to the right, with an inquiring expression.

Brynna smiled with pride at Sam's compliment.

Still dressed in her khaki uniform, hair tamed into a tight French braid, Brynna stood shoulder to shoulder with the mare. Her red hair blended with Penny's copper chestnut mane.

"Thanks," Brynna said. "She's a good girl."

Penny didn't look blind. The large brown eyes that dominated her face weren't cloudy and her face wasn't scarred. Sam couldn't help wondering how Penny had lost her sight.

Brynna held the leather shank attached to the mare's halter. She crooned as she stroked Penny's neck. When the mare turned to rub her face against Brynna's chest, a tiny brass nameplate glittered on the side strap of the polished halter.

The rest of the horses on River Bend Ranch made do with rope or nylon halters and lead ropes, but Penny had been pampered like a pet, Sam thought.

And it showed. Even though she lived in a world of darkness, the mare seemed happy.

"Don't look a bit scared," Dad said.

"She doesn't," Gram echoed. "Why, look at her listening to me."

"She's heard Wyatt's voice before, but not yours," Brynna explained. "Why don't you come over and let her say hello?"

Gram was dressed in muddy-kneed jeans and gardening gloves. That morning she'd mentioned that the Farmer's Almanac said today was a good day for weeding a spring vegetable garden, so that was probably what she'd been doing before.

Since Gram was as grubby as she ever got, it was kind of funny that she touched her hair, as if the mare would notice the tendrils straggling loose from her gray bun. As soon as she'd stripped off the gloves, Gram approached the mare and held both hands flat beneath her nose.

"No food, sweetie," Gram told Penny. "But I've got some baking apples inside and I just might find a snack for you later."

Sam laughed and the mare's head rose, ears pricked in her direction. When Ace gave a low nicker, Penny answered and tugged against the leather shank.

"Be nice to have another redhead on the place," said Pepper. The lanky cowboy from Idaho had gotten his nickname because of his chili pepper–colored hair. "But that pasture's sure getting crowded."

"Wyatt and I talked about that," Brynna said. She nodded toward her husband. "With Buff going back to town for the summer and Dark Sunshine going into the barn corral, we figured it wouldn't be too full."

Sam glanced at the ten-acre pasture.

Strawberry, Tank, and Amigo stood at the fence. The roan, bay, and gray-muzzled sorrel had been on the ranch the longest. They appeared eager to examine the newcomer.

Nike, Buff, and Jeepers-Creepers stood nearby. They glanced toward the bridge, but they didn't move off even a step.

Popcorn and Dark Sunshine, the two captive mustangs, stayed at the rear of the pasture, near the run-in shed. They kept their eyes fixed on the people and horses in the ranch yard.

Both mustangs were familiar with people, but cautious. Popcorn, a tall albino, could be ridden by experienced riders. Dark Sunshine, the golden buckskin in foal to the Phantom, allowed Sam to lead and pet her.

Still, they were wary of the trailer and the new horse. Both mustangs must have remembered a time when their safety depended on vigilance and staying well within the herd.

Sam mentally counted up the horses. Twelve, including Sweetheart, who was still kept in the barn corral, plus Ace. When Buff left for town and Sweetheart and Dark Sunshine switched homes while the buckskin awaited the birth of her foal, the ten-acre pasture would stay at a saddle herd of ten horses. It would be a sociable, but not crowded new home for Penny.

As Ace took a step forward, Sam imagined she heard the baggie rustle in her saddlebag. Sam glanced at Dad. The things she needed to tell him were piling up. She needed his advice, but he was staring at Brynna, obviously enjoying her pleasure in bringing Penny home.

As Brynna rubbed her mare's neck, Sam caught the glint of her wedding ring. For the first time in weeks, Sam felt more than annoyed by her stepmother.

It wasn't jealousy or frustration at the way a new person changed life in their household. Sam thought for a few seconds. Honestly, she felt a little disloyal. To Mom.

And yet, there was Brynna, arms around the neck of the wild horse she loved.

Sam sighed. If she couldn't have Mom . . .

"Sam, I hope you'll help me watch out for Penny," Brynna said suddenly.

"Of course," Sam blurted.

"Careful what you sign on for," Dad said. "The mare's had some bad times."

"What happened?" Sam asked, focusing on the copper mustang. "It's something to do with her blindness, isn't it?"

Brynna nodded. "She was adopted by a family in California before I came to work at Willow Springs. Right away, they trained her to saddle. She was doing well, they said, until she developed the habit of rearing."

Brynna rumpled the mare's mane in affectionate disapproval.

"I'd guess it was from being held back by someone

with heavy hands," Brynna said. "Even now, when she's ridden in company, she wants to be in front. Anyway, the family—" Brynna broke off, shaking her head. "They took her to a professional horse trainer."

"That doesn't sound like such a bad idea," Sam said.

"They didn't check out his credentials very well, because his 'solution' was to encourage the rearing. Then, once she was up, he'd force her over backward and jump clear."

Sam gasped. Even a small horse like Penny was a heavy animal. They were only balanced, really, on all four feet. Sam imagined the terror of the fall, the pain of the impact, and the disorientation that would follow.

"Poor Penny," she said.

"I've heard of doin' that as a last resort," Pepper admitted.

Brynna nodded, looking sad.

"So have I, and it cured Penny, but not in the way they'd hoped. She came home with bad habits she'd never shown before. Shying, refusing to leave her stall . . ."

"She was afraid," Sam said.

"That's what they thought at first," Brynna said. "But they coddled her, gave her lots of affection and sugar cubes. Nothing helped."

Penny stamped a hoof. She pulled at her lead, totally bored with the conversation.

Sam dismounted and let the mare touch noses with Ace, while Brynna continued.

"Kind of in despair, they checked with BLM," Brynna went on. "They'd had her for almost a year, so they were about to get title to her. I was at Willow Springs, by then, and asked a vet to check her out. He took one look at the scars on the back of Penny's head and suspected the worst. Then he did some tests, and discovered the frequent impact had damaged both optic nerves."

"So she was shying because she couldn't see," Sam said. "And they didn't want her anymore."

Brynna shrugged. "They wanted her, but out of pity. Once they got title to her, they planned to put her down. They thought it was too cruel to let her live."

"I'm saying it was guilt," Dad insisted. "They couldn't stand seein' what they'd done."

Right now, Penny didn't look the least bit pitiful. She gave a low neigh and danced in place. Her neck curved toward the ten-acre pasture as if she'd march right over to investigate the horses she could smell and hear.

Instead, Brynna led Penny toward the pipe corral the hands had set up next to the saddle horse pasture.

"Anyway, I couldn't stand to see them put her down," Brynna said. "And it was a good decision to adopt her. Penny's still the most collected, responsive horse I've ever ridden.

"The others will probably try to crowd her, even though there's a fence between them," Brynna went on. "I think she'll stay back, but she could get a few nips and mock kicks, if she's not careful. We just need to watch a while and see that it doesn't go any further than that, okay?"

"Sure," Sam said.

Sam turned Ace into the big pasture as Brynna opened the gate and walked inside the pipe corral leading Penny. Just as Brynna had predicted, the saddle horses ignored Ace and rushed toward Penny.

"Strawberry, you're not the boss of the world. Now get back," Sam said when the red roan mare flattened her ears and lashed her tail at the new horse.

"Tank, she can tell you're tall," Brynna scolded the bald-faced bay when he tried to sling his head over Penny's withers.

After five minutes of crowding the rails, the other horses turned their tails toward Penny, then, noticing Dad had put feed into their mangers, loped away.

"I think she'll be fine," Sam said, glancing over her shoulder as they left the pasture.

"So do I," Brynna said. Still, her tone was hesitant until she added, "But you have good equine instincts, that's why I want your help."

Sam draped her loaded saddlebags on the front porch rail. Mom's note rustled in her pocket. When she straightened, Sam noticed Brynna was still staring at her.

"No problem," she assured her stepmother, and she meant it, as far as Penny was concerned.

She glanced back at the pasture as she lifted Ace's tack.

She'll be fine, Sam told herself, and when Dad approached smiling as she hefted the saddle and kept walking toward the barn, she decided there was no reason to wait.

"Nice little horse, isn't she?" Dad asked.

"Yeah," Sam said. "But Dad, there's something we need to talk about before dinner. Something serious."

Chapter Six ๛

Hurrying, Sam hung her saddle on its rack in the tack room. She shook out her saddle blanket and draped it over the cantle to air. Next, she wiped her bit and bridle and put them away, then she hesitated in the doorway.

Overhead, wild pigeons cooed as they strolled the big wooden beams. Sweetheart, Gram's aged pinto, made careful chewing noises, using worn, old teeth to grind her grain.

Dad sat on a hay bale in the middle of the barn, waiting. Dad was rarely still. There was always work to do, he said, but Sam remembered how Dallas, their foreman, had described Dad when he was polishing leather to a high sheen. *Peaceful as a church*, Dal had said. That was how her father looked right now.

Dad hadn't turned on the overhead light in the barn. He just sat there, face shaded by his gray Stetson, hands linked and hanging between his knees, as he watched Sweetheart enjoy her feed. He looked so contented, Sam regretted what she had to do.

Maybe she wouldn't tell him. At least not everything. She'd show him the note, but not mention the gunman.

That thought made her stomach tighten. *Not* mention a man with a gun?

But Jen could be right. The hermit at Snake Head Peak might be poor and hungry, just hunting his dinner instead of buying it at the supermarket.

"What's on your mind, honey?" Dad said when he spotted her. He patted a space beside him on the hay bale. "Come sit down and tell me."

Sam reached into her pocket, withdrew the note, and handed it to him. Dad took it. He blinked, then his eyebrows rose in reaction. He must have recognized the stationery, Sam thought, because he removed his hat and ran one hand over his hair before he unfolded it.

Sam held her breath as Dad read it then released it when he looked up.

He left the paper open on his knees, then smoothed it out with a lingering pass of his palm.

Sam fidgeted with impatience.

Why didn't Dad slap his forehead and wonder

aloud why he hadn't seen, long ago, that Mom's death was linked with the fate of the wild horses?

Instead, his gaze dropped, and he read the list over again with a faint smile.

Finally, he asked, "Where'd you find this?"

"In the button box," Sam answered, though it wasn't what she'd expected him to say.

Dad nodded, not as if he'd put it there or anything; but more as if he wasn't surprised.

"So, what do you think?" she asked.

"It'll make a nice keepsake. That part about her tryin' sunsuits on you, and getting ham and Swiss cheese. That's my favorite sandwich, you know, and that Darton Deli has long since gone out of business."

"But Dad!" The words came out like a cry. "What about the horses? Mom was worried about the mustangs."

"Sure. She always was," he admitted. "Some hunters thought horses were pushy and ran off the game. Louise read up on it and saw it was almost never so." He nodded slowly. "I think that's what this is about. She'd been doin' some reading and just wanted to remember to tell me about it."

Sam stared at her father's calm brown eyes. Above them, she noticed the strip of white skin on his forehead, where his cowboy hat blocked the sun.

"Dad, I don't think that's all it was," Sam insisted.

He started to speak, then stopped and considered her with a pitying expression.

"Maybe not," he said.

He was no help at all! Dad knew more about Mom than anyone else in the world, but he was blind to the conspiracy she'd uncovered.

Dad stood up, slowly. He braced his hands against the small of his back and stretched. She knew he was tired, but Dad was always tired. This was important.

"Let's ask your gram what she thinks," he said.

Sam's spirits rose. Gram and Mom hadn't just been mother-in-law and daughter-in-law. They'd been close friends. One reason Gram wanted to teach Sam to bake lasagna was because it was Mom's special dish.

And it was on this list. Gram would like that. The list might trigger Gram's memory of something Mom was worried about, too. Sam had noticed that a lot of talking went on when women spent time together in a kitchen.

"Okay," Sam agreed. She was ready to do it right now. She stood abruptly.

"We'll ask Brynna about the wild horse part of it," Dad added.

Sam drew a deep breath and turned to face Dad. For a minute, he didn't look sympathetic. He looked skinny, tanned, and stubborn.

Sam was equally stubborn. "Why should we ask her? She didn't know Mom."

"As a biologist, I'd say she knows a fair amount about wildlife."

Sam crossed her arms. Dad's understatement was meant to make her feel dumb. Of course she knew Brynna was a biologist, and she admired her knowledge about animals. She'd never forget Brynna's calm interest when she'd observed a young cougar atop Linc Slocum's buffet table.

But Sam was pretty sure Dad was pointing out that if Sam wasn't satisfied with his opinion of the list, they had an in-house wildlife expert.

She and Dad faced each other, neither willing to break off their locked stares.

Sam heard a rustling, flapping sound from outside. Dad must have heard it, too.

"Before we go up to the house for dinner, I want you to fix that blue tarp I've got covering the extra lumber. Weight it down around the edges with rocks or something. We don't want it blowing away and we sure don't want that wood getting rained on and ruined."

Sam nodded absently. A light breeze blew through the ranch yard, but there'd only been a few wispy clouds all day and it didn't smell like rain was waiting in the sky. Dad was just assigning extra work to distract her.

"Okay, I will," she agreed anyway.

Dad folded the list along its creases, but he didn't hand it over right away.

He held it loosely, and his chest rose higher than usual, with each breath. Was it sappy to think Dad was realizing Mom had touched the list? That some molecule from her hand still lingered there?

Okay, Sam told the critical half of her brain, *then I'm sappy*.

She wanted Dad to remember Mom and tell her everything.

"You know why she made lists?" Dad asked suddenly.

Sam shook her head.

"She loved this place." Dad's arms spread wide, taking in the ranch, desert, and mountains. "She'd go out to run some errand and get so distracted, she'd come back empty-handed." Dad looked down, chuckling and shaking his head. "I got frustrated with her, I'll admit. But she didn't care. She'd toss her hair and inform me that she was making up for lost time, for all the years she didn't know the high desert existed."

Dad pulled his hat back on. He tugged it so low on his brow, Sam couldn't see his eyes at all. She was pretty sure he did it on purpose. Dad was hiding tears. That's probably why his voice turned harsh, too.

"I'll check Penny before I go in," he snapped. "That's just what we need around here. A blind mustang. Another useless mouth to feed. Tell your gram I'll be up in time for dinner."

For a second, Dad was outlined in the barn door and his shoulders looked stiff. Sam watched him go.

She should go look for that flapping tarp. She could still hear it. Instead, she thought about the saddlebags she'd dumped on the front porch, with the shell casing inside. What if someone stepped on it and crushed it?

A careful analyst could probably still lift a fingerprint, but why take a chance?

Sam darted toward the house. She'd take the saddlebags and baggie upstairs before dinner and worry about that tarp later.

"Lands," Gram said, as she read Mom's list after dinner. "I'd forgotten Dallas went through a stage with his arthritis where he rubbed chili oil on his joints. Louise knew it didn't do any good, but she bought it for him and all the while harassed him to go see a doctor."

Sam glanced at the faces around the table. Gram and Dad looked soft-eyed and nostalgic. Brynna looked worried.

"Samantha, we'll make lasagna this weekend, I promise," Gram said. "Louise had such a knack for it. Especially the sauce. Anyone can just layer noodles, meat, and cheese, but she crushed the herbs with a mortar and pestle —" Gram broke off to look around the kitchen. "I have it here somewhere—and it gave the oregano and basil such zip."

Sam shifted in her chair. Gram was pleased by the memory, and that was fine, but the kind of memories she'd hoped to stir up about her mother didn't have much to do with lasagna.

"I want you to take a look, too," Dad said, sliding the note toward Brynna.

Startled, Brynna touched her chest as if to ask, *Me?*

A faint satisfied smile touched her lips before she began reading.

"I know this guy! Caleb Sawyer," she said, tapping the paper.

Sam rose from her chair and turned her head to read the words Brynna had pointed out. Someplace between number three and five, Sam thought, the parts about antelope season, the BLM, and Caleb's criminal record.

"Caleb Sawyer," Dad said, nodding with recognition.

"I haven't thought of that scoundrel for years," Gram said.

"*Is* he a criminal?" Sam asked.

"I don't know about that," Brynna said. "But he's always complaining that his land is overrun with mustangs. He's more of a nuisance than anything."

Sam's mind stampeded with possibilities. Was Caleb Sawyer making complaints about horses so he could shoot them? Or was he really trying to hunt the antelope grazing alongside the horses? What had Mom thought?

"His spread does border BLM land," Dad said.

"He's been claiming horse trespass for as long as I can remember."

Dad looked thoughtful for a few seconds, then his gaze swung back to Sam. "I want you to stay away from there."

Sam sat back in her chair. Now she really couldn't tell Dad about the rifle shots.

"I will," she said. "But why?"

"He's always been kind of an odd duck," Dad said.

Gram and Brynna looked at each other, trying to wring more meaning out of Dad's words.

"I don't know what he's done before, but I can tell you it's Linc Slocum that keeps him stirred up, now," Brynna said.

"Lands," Gram muttered. "That Linc is never happy unless everyone around him is miserable."

"How are they . . ." Sam searched for a suitable word. "Connected?"

Brynna bit her bottom lip for a minute. "I've never asked Linc about it, but Caleb always brings him up. As if Linc Slocum gives him credibility."

Sam's mind raced. Linc Slocum was always trying to put some unscrupulous plan in motion. His schemes were often cruel and dangerous. He'd tried to raise Brahma bulls and bison, and both plans had endangered people's lives and left the animals miserable. And ever since he'd moved to northern Nevada with his millions of dollars, he'd longed to own the Phantom.

There'd been a wild white stallion on this range for as long as anyone could remember. The horse—or horses, to be sensible—had become a legend, and Linc Slocum, who was used to buying everything he wanted, couldn't stand it that the stallion had no price.

Could Caleb Sawyer somehow fit into his obsession to have her horse?

"I don't get it," Sam said. "What do you mean, Linc gives him credibility?"

Brynna thought a minute. "You know, Caleb stays out there at Snake Head Peak all alone, but he brings up Linc as if he knows him. Like, 'Linc says I have a legitimate gripe against BLM 'cause they put horses before people' or 'Linc says that white stud—'"

"What?" Sam gasped.

Both Gram and Dad stared at Brynna as if she'd made a mistake.

"It's the Phantom he's talking about," Sam said.

"Not necessarily," Gram began.

"Oh, yes it is," Sam insisted.

She couldn't explain why she was so sure. Only she, Jen, and the shooter had seen the Phantom at Antelope Crossing.

"It could be," Brynna admitted, "but all he's said to me is that the stallion is trespassing."

"It would still be against the law to shoot him, wouldn't it?" Sam said.

"Of course," Brynna snapped. "But that's not what Caleb has in mind. I'm sure he just wants compensation." Brynna gave an angry smile. "In other words, money, for the free meals the horses have had on his land."

Brynna was wrong.

But Sam couldn't tell her so, if she ever wanted to go there again to investigate.

"So you're not going to report him to the sheriff?" Sam asked.

"What in heaven's name for?" Gram asked. "There's plenty of greed to go around since Slocum moved in."

"If greed were a jailin' offense, Heck Ballard wouldn't do much else," Dad said.

If she mentioned the rifle, Sheriff Hector Ballard would be involved, Sam decided. And soon.

For tonight, she'd say no more. But she'd bet the sheriff would welcome her and Jen as witnesses. He'd take fingerprints from the shell casing, too. And then, when he read the evidence in her mother's note, every puzzle piece would fit.

And Sheriff Ballard would arrest the hermit of Snake Head Peak.

Chapter Seven ◎

Sam was finishing up washing the dinner dishes. For once, she had no homework, but she couldn't stop thinking about Journalism.

She let the hot water run over her hands, remembering the burning blush she'd felt. She really wanted to be photo editor. Even more than that, she wanted to prove she deserved it.

She'd like to call Jen, but it was hard to have a private conversation when the only telephone was in the kitchen, next to the living room where Brynna, Dad, and Gram sat watching television. Still, she'd give it a try.

She had to convince Jen to stay quiet about the gunman. She might also confide what Rachel had said in class, before it became gossip.

And it would. Sam just knew it.

Rachel Slocum was not only her Daddy's princess; she was one of the most popular girls at Darton High. Sam couldn't figure that out.

Rachel was model-sleek. She pampered herself with the finest makeup and clothes. So, sure, she looked great. But Rachel also looked down on everyone.

After her cheerleader friend had dropped Journalism for the spring semester, Rachel had allowed Cammy, a freshman girl with blond ringlets, to be her follower.

Every day Rachel encouraged Cammy to sneak out of class and buy her a diet Coke from the machine in the teachers' lunchroom. Cammy did it, though she'd been caught twice and punished.

It was a mystery why, but Rachel and her boyfriend Kris Cameron were popular. Even if they weren't admired, they were cool. That made every word they uttered instantly important.

Sam was groaning in self-pity and Blaze the Border collie had answered her with a canine moan, when the phone rang.

Sam dried her hand and answered it.

"Like to talk to Brynna, Sam."

When she heard the voice of Luke Ely, she knew something exciting was about to happen.

Luke was Jake's dad. He was tall, handsome for

a father, and he was chief of the volunteer fire department. But he wasn't a sociable man.

"I'll get her," Sam said. But she couldn't help asking, "Is something wrong?"

"Just got an odd phone call," he said, and if a voice could hold a shrug, his did. "Nothing that you and Jake couldn't handle, come to think of it, but it kinda falls in Brynna's line of work, not mine."

"Hang on," Sam said, motioning to Brynna and handing over the receiver.

Sam stood next to Brynna, watching her with such intensity, Brynna finally turned her back so that she could concentrate while she talked with Jake's dad.

"We were just talking about Caleb Sawyer," Brynna said, at last.

Ohmygosh. Sam's heartbeat quadrupled in speed.

"Some kids *and* mustangs?" Brynna asked as she turned to watch Sam's reaction.

Sam felt herself frowning, but she hoped she didn't look guilty.

She must not have, because right away, Brynna was talking again to Luke.

"So, basically, he's complaining about trespassing again, and he called you because he couldn't get any satisfaction from me?" Brynna listened a minute, then laughed. "So he expected you to squirt them with a fire hose? It doesn't sound like anything that can't wait for tomorrow," Brynna began, then broke off to listen.

She looked at Sam, then glanced up at the kitchen clock.

"I do have a new horse I need to keep an eye on," Brynna said, and Sam wondered why it sounded like Brynna was making an excuse. "Okay, Luke, thanks. I'll have her ready when he gets here."

Sam's nerves thrummed with excitement. Brynna's expression looked hesitant, but Sam was pretty sure she wasn't in trouble.

"What?" she asked, impatiently.

"Wait here," Brynna said, and walked into the living room.

Sam tiptoed close to the connecting door, trying to listen to whatever had Brynna checking with Dad.

The buzz of television laughter covered most of the conversation, but Sam heard a few words clearly.

"She's determined to go out there whether you want her to or not. At least if she goes with Jake, in a truck . . ."

All at once the voice seemed closer, so Sam took a long step back to where Brynna had left her. She laced her fingers together and tried to look patient and angelic as Brynna returned.

"There's no use wasting my breath if you heard everything," Brynna said as the door swung shut behind her. "I didn't," Sam insisted. "Just something about Jake and a truck."

For an instant Brynna looked skeptical. Then she nodded.

"Okay. Caleb Sawyer called Luke Ely complaining that there were wild horses on his property right this minute. . . ."

Sam rose on her toes with excitement until Brynna motioned her to settle down.

"And he mentioned that there were two kids on his property earlier today. I don't suppose you'd know anything about that, so I'm not going to ask."

Sam swallowed hard, glad she was facing Brynna instead of Dad. Dad would have jumped to the correct conclusion, instantly.

"He wanted Luke to come chase the horses off with a fire truck siren. He's not running any cattle," Brynna said. "That makes me wonder why he's so obsessed with the trespass issue. It could just be he's cranky, but I'm wondering if something else is going on."

Sam felt a little puff of pride. Brynna was discussing this with her, instead of with Dad.

"A siren," Sam said. "That's not a real normal approach to a wild horse problem."

"Exactly," Brynna agreed. "Just the same, I'll send someone out tomorrow morning. Right now, though, Luke suggested that you and Jake go out and take a look."

Sam hugged herself with excitement, then whispered, "And Dad said it was okay?"

Brynna held her hand out and tipped it from side to side. "Sort of," she said quietly. "But don't do anything silly or you'll get us both in trouble."

"I'll be an angel," Sam promised.

Blaze jumped up from his nap on the kitchen floor. He stared in the direction of the bridge, as if he could see through the walls.

"That must be Jake," she said.

"Get a sweatshirt," Brynna ordered.

"It's not—"

"Angels do as they're told," Brynna said, eyebrows arched in reprimand.

"Right."

Sam ran upstairs and yanked her green Darton High sweatshirt from the bottom of a stack of clean laundry, causing a clothing avalanche. She stampeded back downstairs so fast, Jake still hadn't knocked at the door.

Then she saw why.

In the glow from the porch light, Brynna was showing off Penny. Holding the screen door so it didn't slam and startle the mare, Sam watched.

It was kind of weird that Jake was so much taller than Brynna. He always said he was six-foot-one-inch tall, but she'd thought he was exaggerating. Standing next to Brynna like that, he looked almost like a man.

Of course, he destroyed the illusion by snorting, "If it's not the tagalong kid."

"Shut up," Sam requested as she jogged down the front porch steps.

"Samantha, be nice," Brynna reprimanded patiently.

"He started it," Sam said.

"I guess I should actually thank you two," Brynna said, looking from Sam to Jake. "I'll never feel old, because you'll never stop acting like children."

Jake squared his shoulders, but didn't answer back.

"Penny looks good. I'd like to see her in action," he said, trying to sound mature. Then he jingled his truck keys like a lure and said to Sam, "Let's go."

Since Jake shared the truck with his brothers, it was usually cluttered, despite the fact that he was a pretty neat guy. Tonight it was worse than usual. A huge mound of stuff hid the passenger's side floor.

"What is all this?" she asked.

"Don't worry about it," Jake said as they rumbled across the River Bend Bridge. Then he glanced over and gave a short laugh. "Go ahead and put your feet down, Brat. You won't hurt anything."

As they drove through the darkness, Sam thought the excursion was even more fun because it was a school night. In theory, she should be home studying, but she hadn't even had to beg to escape.

"How's Star?" Sam asked.

The paint filly Jake had caught on Indian lands, then ridden in a cross-country race, was one of the neatest horses Sam had ever known.

"Fine, I guess," Jake said, but Sam noticed his hands tightened on the steering wheel.

"You 'guess'?" Sam said, but Jake ignored her.

"We're supposed to head toward Antelope Pass," he said. "And turn left on some dirt road."

"Jake, why are you just guessing how Star is?"

"I turned her loose, back where she came from."

Sam didn't know what to say.

Jake switched on the truck radio. The reception wasn't very good. She made out a country tune, but not its lyrics.

"After all your hard work . . ."

Sam pictured Jake running through the night after the horse. Jake sticking to Star's pinto back through a watery bucking frenzy. Jake, hair streaming like a warrior, riding Star at a full gallop across the range.

"Was it because Witch was jealous?" Sam asked. She imagined Jake's big black mare threatening the small pinto. "Or because you won't have time to work with Star this summer?" She took a second guess when he didn't respond but he just gave a slight shake of his head.

Sam waited a full minute before she finally shouted, "Jake! Why did you set her loose?"

"The point wasn't to get a new horse." Jake pressed his shoulders against the seat back, trapping his buckskin-bound hair behind him. "I was supposed to show some adult skills and I did."

"I know," Sam said, knowing her voice sounded weak.

The radio's static grew too loud to speak over, but

Jake didn't turn it off.

Sam was glad. Something about what Jake said disturbed her. As they drove toward Antelope Pass, she considered telling him about her mother's note.

Maybe later, she thought. As the static faded and a chirpy voice praised a new brand of chewing gum, another idea crossed her mind.

"Hey, maybe Star will go back to the Phantom!"

Jake shrugged, but Sam thought something like jealousy crossed his face.

Five minutes later, Jake hadn't given a single indication he was irritated. Then, he slammed on the brakes.

"This is stupid. I can't get over there without ripping out the oil pan on this truck."

The truck idled as they stared across the rocky, pitted terrain.

Sam didn't see any grass-tufted pools of water shining in the headlights' beams.

"Is this the right way?" Sam asked.

"This is how Dad told me to go," Jake said. "But since you're a ninth-grade expert on everything . . ." Jake's sarcasm trailed off as he watched her. "Do you know another way?"

Sometimes Sam thought Jake's tracking skill was related to psychic ability. Not that she believed in mind reading, exactly, but now, as he'd watched her, Jake's whole attitude had changed. He seemed to know she'd been out here today.

So she tried to sound totally casual.

"On horseback, I think you can cross Aspen Creek, then ride up toward Snake Head Peak and get there."

Jake stared out the windshield, leaning forward until his chest pressed the steering wheel.

On the horizon, blacker than the night sky, Sam saw the rock formation that looked like a snake.

Cautiously, Jake eased the car ahead, then turned right on a dirt road that was little more than a trail cut by hooves.

How had Mom driven out here in her clumsy VW bus? Sam puzzled over the question until Jake stopped again.

"There they are," he said.

After a few impatient minutes, Sam spotted the herd. Night light made them all shades of gray. She couldn't find the Phantom or identify any individual mustangs, but there were about twenty horses, the right number for the Phantom's band.

"They're on his property, all right," Jake observed.

On the hermit's property, he must mean. That meant trouble for the horses. How could Jake sound so unconcerned?

"Don't tell Brynna," Sam said. "Promise me."

"If she asks, of course I'll tell her," Jake said.

"Look, they're not hurting anything. That Caleb guy isn't running any cattle and the pronghorn don't mind sharing, so why should you tell?"

"Because Brynna and my dad trusted me to do this," Jake said. His tone indicated he had no choice. "When people, like, respect you, you can either disappoint them or measure up."

Gosh, Sam, don't you know anything? Jake didn't say it, but he might as well have, and his superior attitude made her mad.

"Wait. How do you know the pronghorn don't mind sharing?" Jake asked, giving her a suspicious glance.

Sam ignored his question. She was still stuck on him bragging about how much Brynna trusted him.

"How do you stand yourself," Sam asked, "being so mature and all?"

Jake didn't rise to the bait. Instead he asked, "Are you trying to pick a fight?"

She gestured as if brushing aside his question, because suddenly she'd realized she had to ask his opinion about something important.

"Do you think wild horses compete with antelope for food?" she blurted.

He was quiet for a minute, not quite ready to give up their squabble, but Sam knew he'd think about what she'd asked.

"No. They eat different stuff most of the year," Jake said. "Do you think Caleb wants the horses out of here because of the antelope?"

"Maybe," she told him. "I've heard he's a poacher. If he hunts pronghorn year-round, he might be worried that the horses' grazing area overlaps. Don't you think?"

"Where'd you hear he was a poacher?"

Sam was about to show him her mother's note, when the horses began to drift away, soundless as smoke.

The flat grassland looked bare for a minute. Then something big appeared. Headlights stabbed through the darkness and moonlight rolled on a windshield.

Was it Caleb Sawyer? Didn't hermits stay home? That's what made them hermits, right?

The headlights bounded over the rough terrain, coming closer.

What if the hermit was driving out to see if Luke Ely had sent someone? What if he came right up to Jake's truck and looked inside?

Sam thought of the shell casing.

If this was the shooter, he might have seen her gathering evidence and carefully bagging it. A clammy warmth settled over her as she realized Jake was accelerating, actually hurrying to meet the other vehicle.

"Stop!" Sam urged. "Don't go over there."

What if Caleb Sawyer had used binoculars to see her clearly? If he drove right up beside them, she just knew he'd still have that rifle.

"Sam, what's wrong with you? Don't grab my arm when I'm driving," Jake snapped. "I might crash."

"You *will* crash, if you keep going toward him, 'cause that guy's got a gun."

"Sam, three-quarters of the ranchers around here have rifles. I've got one at home. Relax."

"But he uses it!"

"What are you talking about?"

To convince Jake to stop being foolhardy, she'd have to tell him the truth.

"Today," she blurted. "I saw him use it today. He was trying to shoot horses and he wasn't trying to miss me, okay? He doesn't care if he hurts people."

"Mighta been nice if you'd mentioned this to me before, Brat," Jake commented in a strained but level tone.

"I'm *mentioning* it now," Sam moaned. "Please, let's get out of here before he recognizes me!"

Jake cranked the steering wheel hard right and spun the truck around. The fact that he'd taken her warning to heart should have made her feel better. Instead, she was even more scared.

Sam leaned forward as if it would help the truck speed across the range. Suddenly the tires hit a series of mud ruts, which had dried into ridges that were as hard as concrete. They bounced in jerky jolts until the truck veered right, jarring Sam's head against the passenger window with a sharp crack.

As if she could hide from the pain, Sam closed her eyes. The darkness welcomed her. If she could only stay there, for a minute . . .

Chapter Eight ❧

Sam felt dizzy.

She heard a loud stomp. Was it Jake putting on the emergency brake?

A click. Jake releasing his seat belt?

Then Sam sensed something scrabbling toward her. Her eyes popped wide open.

Jake loomed over her in the dark truck.

"Are you okay? That was your head hitting the window, wasn't it? I don't even believe this."

"I'm fine," she said, pushing at his chest. "Back off, can't you? Is he still after us?"

Jake ignored her question and her shoves.

"You're supposed to avoid another blow to the head," he said as one hand pushed aside her hair and his fingers explored her temple.

It was creepy, the way he felt gently for cuts or blood. It was stupid, too. Those injuries would mean nothing if the hermit caught up with them.

"Forget about my head, look!"

The headlights were still coming. They cut crazy, slashing patterns through the darkness. Sam squinted as a spotlight shone from the top of the blocky, black-and-white vehicle. Was it stopping?

The light was so blindingly bright, she didn't see the figure until it was at the driver's side window.

"You kids okay?" Sheriff Ballard shouted.

Sam touched her chest, trying to slow the thud of her pounding heart. This must be how a rabbit felt when it had been chased by a coyote, then escaped into its burrow.

Jake opened the door on his side of the truck.

"Jake Ely, right?"

Sam guessed the sheriff recognized Jake for the tracking help he'd given the police once.

"Yes, sir," Jake said. He didn't look surprised when the sheriff shone the beam of his flashlight inside.

Sam squinted against the brightness. With her eyes almost closed, she said, "I'm Samantha Forster."

"Wyatt's girl, and you've got your seat belt on, so that jouncing didn't hurt you much. Am I right?"

Before Sam could say anything, Jake did.

"She banged her head against the window."

And here came the flashlight again. Sam closed her

eyes against light so bright the blood vessels in her eyelids shone sizzling red. Her head felt fine, but her retinas would probably never be the same.

"Looks okay," the sheriff said. "But you'll want to tell your dad you got a bump, make sure nothin' comes of it."

"I will," Sam promised. That was a conversation she wasn't looking forward to. She'd just hope she didn't have to have it in front of Jake.

He was as protective as a bear with one cub, and just about as easy to reason with. Sam started to shake her head at the silly comparison, but when she did, she felt dizzy all over again.

At least Jake wasn't watching when she winced.

"I notice your rack," the sheriff said, nodding at the gun rack that spanned the truck's back window. "Got a rifle in here?"

"No," Jake said. His face stayed expressionless, but Sam heard the insulted tone in his voice and Sam knew Jake thought he was being accused of something.

Sheriff Ballard must have noticed that tone, too, but he didn't try to make Jake feel better. With his shaggy brown hair, mustache, and alert eyes, the sheriff gave the appearance of a trapper, waiting patiently for Jake to step into a snare.

"Reason I'm here is on account of an anonymous call saying someone was plinking at wildlife out this way," the sheriff explained.

Sam held her breath for a second. How could there have been a call? She and Jen had been the only ones out here, hadn't they? The hermit wouldn't report himself.

If she didn't tell the sheriff she'd been out here, Jake might. She shot him a quick glance.

Oh, yeah. Jake's eyes said he'd definitely tell.

"There was," Sam admitted.

"Was what?" the sheriff asked.

"Someone shooting at mustangs and antelope," Sam said.

"Did you get a look at him?"

"Not a very good one," Sam admitted. When the sheriff stood there, waiting, she added, "Good enough to know it wasn't anyone I recognized." Still, Sheriff Ballard stayed silent. "It was a man."

"You didn't see a vehicle, I suppose?" the sheriff asked.

"I'm pretty sure there wasn't one, or a horse."

"The call didn't say much, either," the sheriff said. "Not enough to go on. We're having it traced, though, so maybe we'll get something more from the caller."

Sam bit her lip. Could it have been Jen? It would be like her to report something dangerous, but why had she made the report anonymously?

"I saved the shell casing," Sam offered. Both the sheriff and Jake looked at her with amazement. Had she said it wrong? "You know, the brass thing that goes around the bullet?"

"That's the shell casing," Sheriff Ballard said, nodding. "You picked it up?"

"In a plastic baggie," Sam said.

Sheriff Ballard shook his head and laughed. "Just when I get irritated with TV folks for making police work look fun and easy, something like this happens.

"And you still have it?" he asked.

"At home," Sam blurted.

The sheriff chuckled again.

"If I picked you up after school tomorrow, do you think you could give it to me and we could go to my office for a talk?"

Sam almost cheered. This was exactly what she needed. Professional help. She'd bring Mom's note along, too, and since the sheriff was taking her seriously, she'd bet he'd help unravel the snarl of trouble her mother had been investigating.

The sheriff stayed to make sure Jake could back the truck out of the ruts and start home.

Once they were on their way, Sam glanced at the glowing turquoise numbers on her watch. It seemed like forever since she'd left River Bend, but it was only eight thirty.

When she yawned, Jake glanced over at her.

"How's your head?" he asked grimly.

Sam felt so impatient with him, she thought about faking a faint. But that would be a really bad idea.

Jake still blamed himself for the head injury she'd suffered when he was helping her gentle Blackie, the colt who'd grown up to be the Phantom.

"It's fine." Sam sighed, but she could tell Jake was drowning in guilt because he'd been driving, now, when she hit her head again.

They drove in silence for a few minutes and Sam was just beginning to think Jake wasn't going to act paranoid and overly protective when he exploded.

"Are you crazy?" he shouted.

"Why do people keep asking that? Of course I'm—"

"Because you have a one-track mind when it comes to mustangs," Jake said. "Nothing else matters. Think about this: A guy with a gun nearly shoots you and you don't tell anyone?"

"I just told someone," Sam said, crossing her arms and cinching them tightly against each other.

"But you wouldn't have, would you?"

"Oh yeah, right," she snapped, then continued with more than her usual sarcasm. "I was planning to wear that shell casing on a chain around my neck."

"I wouldn't be surprised," Jake muttered. After a few seconds he added, "I don't know Caleb Sawyer. My dad doesn't think he's dangerous, but don't go getting any ideas about knocking on his door and asking him questions."

Arms still crossed, Sam shook her head. Jake really must think she was crazy. She wouldn't do that.

But if she did, it might help answer some questions.

What would she do when she got to Caleb

Sawyer's ranch? Ask if his antelope poaching had somehow caused her mother's death?

"Hey, if you went with me—" Sam broke off when Jake glared at her. "Never mind."

"Sure, 'never mind.' All you're going to tell me is some guy shot at you. That figures."

"I—You didn't ask," she said. "Why are you so mad?"

Jake's head shook in a curt refusal to talk. If she didn't know, his gesture said, he couldn't explain in a hundred years.

Now, River Bend Ranch had come into sight. Sam could see the glow of the front porch light.

Blaze started barking, announcing their arrival, while Sam tried to decide how to keep Jake outside while she went in. That would be important.

Because she wasn't stupid, she'd mention she'd bumped her head, but there was absolutely no reason to tell Dad, Gram, and Brynna about the sheriff. Or the shell casing.

She hadn't been hurt, after all. The gunman had been trying to shoot animals. For sure. After all, when she'd yelled at him, he'd skulked away.

Jake had not been there. He didn't know. And, though she was the one with the head injury, *he* was certifiably insane on the subject of her safety. He could not be allowed to get her family in an uproar.

She'd be in enough trouble without his interference.

Ace neighed a welcome when Jake's truck stopped and Blaze bounded across the River Bend Ranch yard. Sam opened the truck door to escape Jake's glare and her horse continued a conversational nickering.

"Hey, baby," Sam said, smooching at Ace.

She saw a flicker at the kitchen window as a curtain was drawn back, then dropped into place. It would've been perfect if everyone had already been in bed, but her bad luck day was still holding on.

Out of the corners of her eyes, Sam watched. Sure enough, Jake climbed out of the truck as well.

"You don't have to come in," she said pleasantly.

He shrugged and kept walking toward the porch.

Fine, Sam thought. *No more Ms. Nice Guy.*

"I can handle this, Jake."

A cricket chirped, a night bird warbled a question, and Jake still didn't say anything, just stomped his big, stupid boots up the porch, then waited for her to catch up.

With choppy steps, she followed, then stood on the porch, hands on hips, and glared at him.

Jake only looked bored.

"I hate you, Jake Ely," she said.

He had the nerve to smile. "After you, sweet talker," he said, then opened the door and nodded her on through.

When Blaze crowded ahead of her, Sam let him go.

* * *

Any other night, walking into a kitchen that smelled of cinnamon and sugar would feel great.

Not tonight. Instead of finding Gram amid a clutter of rolling pin and waxed paper, she'd hoped Gram would be upstairs, asleep.

She paused in her walnut chopping to smile at them.

"Hello, Jake," Gram said, then peered inside the oven to check the cookies that were already baking. "Thanks for seeing Sam home."

Gram didn't glance at the clock, but the fact that she didn't start filling Jake full of food reminded Sam it was getting late and tomorrow was school.

Jake rubbed the back of his neck. He only did that when he felt awkward. She still had a chance to drive him out of here.

"Yeah Jake, thanks," Sam said. "See you tomor—"

"Unless you'd like to sit for a minute and wait for this first batch of cookies to be done," Gram offered.

Traitor! Sam thought. Gram just couldn't resist feeding people.

"Okay," Jake said. He'd barely lowered himself into a chair when the door between the kitchen and living room swung open.

"Wasn't that Sam? Oh. Hi, Jake."

Brynna wasn't in her robe yet, but her hair hung loose and Dad was right behind her, wearing his socks, without boots.

"Jake," Dad said, nodding.

Jake shifted in discomfort. His cheeks flushed such a dark red, anyone would have thought Dad had forgotten his pants!

Good. Maybe he'd leave after all, Sam thought.

But he didn't. Jake was determined to stay and humiliate her, no matter what.

Gram leaned past Sam to place a plate of warm cookies on the table. She patted Sam's shoulder as she straightened, then took a quick, surprised breath.

"What's this?" Gram said, looking at Sam's temple.

Oh my gosh. Had it swollen? Bruised?

"Just a little bump." Sam struggled to sound casual. "No big deal."

"What happened out there, Jake?" Dad didn't say it like an accusation, either. It was more like Jake had been the adult in charge.

"Oh, it's nice of you to ask *him*, instead of trusting your own daughter!"

"*Did* something happen?" Brynna asked Sam.

Her stepmother's expression flashed between guilt for letting Sam go and professional interest. But at least she wasn't addressing her question to Jake.

"No trouble with the horses," Sam began, but then Jake interrupted.

"She knocked her head against the window—"

"But I'm okay!"

"—when I hit a rut, running from headlights."

"Did that Caleb do something crazy?" Dad's

voice was as low and threatening as Blaze when he growled.

"No," Jake admitted.

Of course, *now* Jake decided to clam up. He lifted his hand a fraction of an inch off the table, gesturing at Sam.

"Samantha?" Dad asked.

She had no choice, so she tried to get everything out without taking a second breath.

"Today when Jen and I were riding out there, just looking for New Moon, we saw some pronghorn mixed in with the Phantom's herd and then all of a sudden, this guy stands up—I don't know if it was Caleb Sawyer, it could've been, I think it was—and he tried to shoot the Phantom."

"The Phantom's band was over at Snake Head Peak?" Brynna asked.

Dad's head whipped around to send Brynna a look. He seemed to be saying, *You're as bad as she is.*

"I mean," Brynna amended her statement, "what were you doing over at Snake Head Peak? Moon's territory was Aspen Creek, and Phantom usually doesn't hang out there."

Dad set his jaw so hard that Sam heard his teeth grind against each other.

He pushed his chair back so hard it screeched, then strode to the door and opened it.

"Thanks for stoppin' by," he told Jake. "I'll take it from here."

"What?" Sam yelped. Was she some problem to be shepherded from one male to the next? She looked to Brynna and Gram for help, but neither said a word.

"Let me get this straight." Dad's voice was so quiet, Sam had to lean forward to hear. "Some fella started shooting near you this afternoon, but you rode home, talked awhile real normal about Penny, had this"—he broke off, hand moving as if it could spin the right word—"private talk with me in the barn—then more talk at dinner—and you didn't think it was important to tell me about a man shooting horses?"

"That's just like lying, Sam," Brynna said, summing up Dad's words.

"It's not! I was going to tell," Sam insisted, but Dad was pacing, ignoring her.

"I even kept the shell casing," she told him.

Dad stopped. Hands on hips, he stared toward the kitchen window. With only darkness outside, could he see anything besides his reflection?

Gram sat silent, shaking her head in disappointment.

"I wanted to tell the sheriff, and I already did," Sam said. "He wants to talk with me tomorrow after school."

Dad still didn't turn to listen.

"Then why," Brynna said, "didn't you tell us?"

"I was afraid you'd be, like, overly protective, and not let me do stuff. . . ."

"Sam, every time you've given good reasons for things you wanted to do, we've worked it out with you," Brynna said.

Dad turned and his expression wasn't angry, just cold.

"Never would have believed it, but you were safer in San Francisco."

Sam felt as if her flesh clamped closer to her bones, as if she could make herself smaller and disappear.

"Dad, no," she said, but he met her eyes, daring her to say she'd ever been within yards of a gunman when she lived in Aunt Sue's city apartment. She hadn't.

"Get up to bed," Dad ordered, and before he could say anything worse, Sam went.

Chapter Nine &

Jow could a horse make her so happy? Penny wasn't even her horse, but she lifted Sam's gloom just by being there.

The blind mare crowded against the fence of the pipe panel pen assembled next to the ten-acre corral and neighed a greeting to Sam.

She kicked up her heels and bolted in a run around her pen, delighted to have human company.

"Hi, Penny," Sam crooned, and her smile widened when the sorrel slid to a stop, listening.

Penny tossed her head, flinging aside her forelock as if it, and nothing else, kept her from seeing.

"You are a pretty girl, and I'd stay to pet you, but I've got to feed the chickens before I leave for school."

When the mare gave a disgusted snort, Sam checked the other horses. They pricked their ears in Penny's direction, looking curious, but nothing more.

Sam smiled. Putting the small pipe corral next to the ten-acre pasture would keep the new horse safe while the others got used to her. So far, it seemed to be working.

Sam's smile broke into a yawn.

Dallas, Pepper, and Ross had ridden out to check for calves at about five thirty. Sam knew because Blaze had been so excited, he'd barked and yapped, awakening her.

She must have dozed again, though, because, by the time she made it downstairs, everyone was up.

Then, she'd discovered that even though she was in trouble, feeding the hens was her only morning chore. Gram and Brynna had offered to do everything else.

Sam couldn't figure it out. The previous night, Brynna had tapped on Sam's door to say she was grounded until further notice. She'd refused to listen to Sam's excuses and warned that Sam would be lucky if there weren't other consequences for keeping such a serious incident secret.

Right now, the Rhode Island Red hens were studying Sam suspiciously, as if they didn't see her every morning of their lives. Each hen was the size of a feathered basketball. As soon as Sam began sprinkling their food on the ground, they forgot caution. They rebounded off her ankles, fighting for the cracked corn, grain, and crumbs of cherry muffins left from breakfast.

Excited by the hens' squabbling, Penny sidled down the fence line. She crossed one hoof over the other with the grace of a dressage horse.

Moving into the darkness didn't frighten her, Sam realized. There must be a lesson in that.

"You and me, Penny," Sam promised the red mustang.

She wouldn't let the unknown scare her, either. She'd missed hundreds of hours of hugging, scolding, and companionable silence with Mom. Now, she had a chance to learn more about Mom's life and no one would stop her.

After all, Dad had stopped short of saying he'd actually send her back to San Francisco. He'd been surprised and shocked, but Brynna had said she was only grounded.

She'd be very careful, but she still had to find out what had happened to Mom.

It was weird the way curiosity and sadness had stirred up long-forgotten moments.

This morning, the tart-sweet aroma of Gram's muffins had brought back a memory of Mom cooking.

In it, Sam felt herself waking from a cozy nap. She remembered toddling into the kitchen to watch Mom roll a pastry cutter through pale dough. Next, in a way Sam had found magical, Mom had woven the dough strips over and under into a lattice crust for a cherry pie.

Sensing her there, Mom had looked up with a smile and beckoned Sam to come closer. And she'd gone, of course.

Sam imagined herself tucked under her mother's arm, safe as a baby bird under its mother's wing.

"Gonna be late if you stay there daydreamin'," Dad warned from the porch.

Sam's head snapped back. She'd almost forgotten she was standing in the middle of the ranch yard, but there stood Dad, dressed for the range. He wore leather chaps already, but he held a coffee cup and a wisp of steam curled into the cool morning air.

"Hope you took care of weighting down that tarp," Dad said. "Supposed to be some weather blowing in this weekend."

Sam glanced at the sky. It was clear and blue.

Dad didn't sound very friendly and he was just trying to remind her she was in trouble.

She'd like to blame Jake for telling on her, but the words had come from her mouth. And no matter how she tried to minimize what had happened, there was that rifle.

Unlike Gram and Brynna, Dad could hold a grudge for weeks. This mistake would crop up in every discussion, because, in his opinion, she'd placed herself in danger and then kept it secret.

He'd grounded her. She wasn't allowed to ride or go anywhere except school and, today only, Sheriff Ballard's office.

Sam sighed as Dad watched, stiff-backed, to see what she'd do next. Grounding, Sam feared, was only the beginning of her punishment.

He'd told her to hurry, and she'd better do it. She could take care of the tarp later. What she couldn't do was be late for school.

As Sam walked back toward the house, a single hen strutted away from the others. Searching for a tasty worm, she'd forgotten the first rule of prey animals.

"Stay with the rest of the flock," Sam cautioned, fluttering her hands at the hen. "Get out there alone and something will eat you."

The hen hopped off a few feet, rejoined the flock, and scratched the dirt with total concentration.

Sam couldn't brush her hands on her jeans before grabbing her coat. Today she wore a black skirt, a crisp white blouse, and little gold earrings. Her auburn hair curved into a shiny cap with a few too many waves and she wore a flick of Brynna's mascara on her eyelashes.

She wanted to look nice for her meeting with the sheriff, but she wasn't sure why.

Dad was still standing in the kitchen when she was ready to leave.

"I want you to think about something today," he said.

Sam nodded and braced herself for more scolding.

"That calf of yours is near a year old and thinks she's a horse. That's natural after livin' with 'em for so long. With the rest of the cattle back down here for summer, it'd be a good time to turn her out."

"Buddy?" Sam said.

Dad nodded. Of course she had no other calf. Buddy had been orphaned on the range and Sam had rescued and bottle-fed her in a cozy barn stall until she could eat grass and live in the ten-acre pasture.

"I know you feature yourself her mama," Dad said with a half smile, "but think about it."

Sam took a shuddering breath. It wasn't like she spent much time petting and playing with Buddy anymore. As the calf had matured, she'd kept more to herself. But every now and then, Buddy came when Sam called and stood for minutes, getting her head rubbed.

"I'll think about it," Sam said.

As she left the house to begin her walk to the bus stop, her eyes found Buddy. In the back of her mind, Sam had always known Buddy would be a range cow.

She'd never thought about brushing and haltering the calf, taking her to a county fair to win best of show, but Buddy was pretty, and she might have won.

Her red-brown coat shone with good health. Her

white face wore an intent expression as it bobbed just above the ground.

"Buddy!" Sam called. "Hey, Buddy!"

The Hereford raised her head to chest level. Her pink nose was shiny as she looked in Sam's direction.

"Here I am, girl." Sam waved a hand.

Buddy sneezed, flicked her tail, then resumed her search for green grass.

A thud and stutter of hooves made Sam's attention shift.

Ears flat and head extended, Strawberry made a short run at Penny, warning her she'd wandered too close to the fences separating them. The blind mustang shied and ran for the opposite side of her pen.

Sam's breath caught as the mare stopped just in time. A collision with that pipe panel would have hurt her badly.

Buddy would be fine, but Sam felt a pinch of worry over Penny. The sorrel mare was settling into her new environment, but her limitations couldn't be ignored. Brynna needed help watching over Penny.

Sam knew she should help. Brynna trusted her horse sense. And she would help, just not now. She had to go to school. Not right after classes, either, because she'd be grilling Sheriff Ballard for information. But soon.

May sunshine had coaxed swaths of dandelions to decorate the grassy quad at Darton High School.

Just like most other students, Sam and Jen were planning to enjoy lunch outside.

Jen wore new pink jeans with a turquoise tee-shirt and pink bows tied to the ends of her braids.

"Nice jeans," Sam told Jen, as they waited in line at the snack bar window.

"On sale at Mix n Match at the mall." Jen dismissed the compliment, but Sam could tell it pleased her. Then Jen made a shy announcement.

"I hope you won't mind riding home on the bus alone today." A smile tugged the corners of her mouth, though Jen looked as if she were trying to suppress it.

"No, I—"

"Because Ryan's giving me a ride home!"

"Wow." Sam forced herself to sound excited.

She didn't share Jen's infatuation with Ryan Slocum. Probably that was a good thing. It would be disastrous if they both had a crush on him.

That would never happen. She didn't trust Ryan Slocum. She knew it wasn't fair to judge him by the rest of his family, but she couldn't help it.

"He said he had errands in town all week, and . . ." Jen paused to sigh. "He might pick me up every day after school."

"Sounds like a romance to me," Sam joked, even though she didn't like the possibility much. She and Jen had their best talks on the long bus rides home.

As they turned with treats in hand, Sam's spirits

perked up. Just for today, Ryan was actually helping her. Now she wouldn't be the one leaving Jen to ride the bus home alone, while she went to talk with Sheriff Ballard.

Being careful not to spill the chocolate milk shake that she called lunch, Sam swerved around a patch of bright yellow dandelions. They reminded her of the daisies Mom had stuck into her braided hair.

Sam pictured her own hair. It was almost long enough to braid. Would it bother Dad if she copied the hairstyle she'd seen in photographs of Mom?

"They're weeds, Samantha," Jen said as Sam tiptoed around more dandelions. "You can step on them."

"Don't want to," Sam chirped, pointing her toes as she danced between them.

"Why are *you* so happy?" Jen asked. She considered Sam in a raised-brow side glance. "I thought you were grounded."

Jen was right. She shouldn't be happy. Misery would probably kick in after today.

Sam glanced at her watch. In less than two hours, Sheriff Ballard would pick her up and take her to the police station. Most people wouldn't see that as a treat, but . . .

"Hello?" Jen said. "Anybody in there?" She pretended to knock on Sam's head, then snatched her hand back as if she'd done something wrong.

"Just spring fever," Sam said. "I think it's affected my brain."

"You shouldn't make jokes like that," Jen whispered. Her tone reminded Sam of yesterday's creepy feeling.

"What did you hear?" Sam demanded, but she knew it was Rachel's gossip.

Jen could have pretended she didn't know what Sam was talking about, but she didn't.

"Rachel's saying—and Cammy is repeating it like an echo—that you're having a delayed reaction to the head injury. Most people don't believe them. It's just the rumor of the week, you know?"

"What kind of 'delayed reaction'?" Sam asked, though part of her didn't really want to know.

Jen puffed her cheeks out like balloons, then sighed. "She says you're having trouble talking—which is obviously not true," Jen said, smiling. "And walking. . . ."

As Sam looked down at her feet, she bumped into one of the big green barrels that served as campus trash cans. At once, she steadied it, to keep it from falling over.

She should have laughed. She tried to, but amusement stuck in her throat. Instead, she glanced around to see if anyone was watching.

"You're no clumsier than usual," Jen diagnosed. "And the other thing, about logic—I know it's because of your mom."

"*What's* because of my mom?"

"Your obsession with the note."

Obsession wasn't a very nice word. Sam bristled, but she couldn't get mad. Jen was the only person on this campus who understood her.

So she tried to explain. "That note is the only key to this mystery."

"Have you considered," Jen said, slowly pushing her glasses up her nose, "that it might not be a mystery?"

"Of course it is," Sam insisted. She shook her head as if she could shake off Jen's doubt. "Look, I've never done one nice thing for my mom. Not that I remember," she hurried to add. "It's almost Mother's Day and finding out about this horse and pronghorn thing, and Mom's death—well, I'm doing it for her."

As she finished, Sam expected sympathy.

Instead, Jen crossed her arms and tapped her toe. She bit her bottom lip, as if fighting for patience.

The bell to end lunch rang. Students hustled by. Still, Jen watched her with judging eyes.

"Or," Jen said, finally, "you could forget the past, and do something nice for your Gram and Brynna."

Sam couldn't draw enough breath to talk past her fury. Jen stood there, twisting one white-blond braid around her finger, ready to take Sam's anger when she could finally dish it out.

"You're my friend. You're supposed to understand." Sam looked around wildly. "I understood your *obsession*, when you were catching Golden Rose and trying to get your parents back together."

"Enough," Jen whispered, and Sam knew she'd gone too far.

Now people were staring. And wondering if what Rachel had said was true, since only a crazy person would be acting like this out in the middle of the quad.

"Fine! Just—fine!" Sam shouted, then stormed off to Journalism.

She took her time, easing off her backpack. She slid the zipper open slowly and extracted a notebook. She centered it on the desk, trying not to look up as Rachel came in, but she couldn't help it.

The short pink dress Rachel wore was strapless, and though she'd tossed a matching sweater over her shoulders, no one was fooled. Rachel was breaking the rules and daring anyone to punish her.

But what else was new, Sam thought.

Rachel was watching her from under lowered eyelids. Sam could feel it, so she was relieved when RJay pushed her toward the class darkroom.

In the eerie light of the darkroom, he said, "I want you for photo editor next year, but you've got to do something to earn it."

"Like what?" Sam's mind spun, trying to shake off the fight with Jen and Rachel's scheme to steal the editorship with gossip.

"Stay awake, and when I throw something your way, think fast," RJay said, and then he left.

Sam stood in the darkroom a moment longer

trying to decide what RJay had meant. He might have been talking about playing catch instead of staffing the school paper.

Guys were entirely too weird, Sam thought as she emerged from the darkroom and almost ran into Cammy.

Cammy was leafing through assignments on a clipboard Mr. Blair had hung on a nail. Although she kept her eyes downcast, she wasn't signing up for anything.

"You really owed Rachel a chance to be on television for that . . ." Cammy's ringlets jiggled as she spun her hand in the air. "That community service thing. Have a horse—"

"Have a *Heart*," Sam corrected.

"Whatever," Cammy's blue eyes rounded in amazement, as if Sam could possibly think accuracy was as important as Rachel's offense. "Rachel deserved to be on TV a lot more than you, you know."

Cammy gave Sam a quick look up and down, then continued. "Rachel was furious, you know. All of spring break, when she was in Paris—she called me from Paris to tell me, even—she was really, really mad."

Cammy gave the clipboard a push and it swayed back and forth on its hook. "Rachel never forgets stuff like that. She's kinda, you know, into payback."

Cammy drifted away before Sam could think of what to say. She refused to give Rachel the satisfaction of panicking, but she couldn't concentrate on

Journalism, or making a list of questions for Sheriff Ballard. She could only imagine Dad sending her back to San Francisco. She wouldn't have to face Rachel's sly hints that something was wrong with her, but her heart would break without Ace and the Phantom, Jen, and, yeah, admit it, she told herself, Jake.

Later, when she told Mr. Blair she felt sick to her stomach, Sam wasn't lying. She took refuge in the girl's lavatory, where it was cool and quiet.

She stared at herself in the mirror.

"Yuck," she commented.

Her cheeks looked white, as if sprayed with a coating of salt. Tears had cut channels that still showed. She stuck her tongue out at her reflection, then glanced toward the bathroom door.

Good thing no one was there. Word would have spread even faster that she was a confirmed psycho.

Maybe she was. What kind of people carried bullet shell casings in their backpacks? Not normal ones.

Sam threw water on her face, then fluffed the dampness out of her bangs.

What was it Gram always said? *This time next year, none of this will matter.*

But it would. Mom's death, and the manner of it, still mattered. Caleb Sawyer and his rifle, aimed directly at the Phantom, mattered.

Right before her eyes, Caleb Sawyer had proven he would take a horse's life.

If Caleb Sawyer had caused Mom's accident, he should pay for it.

Sam looked at her watch. Five more minutes of class. She could maintain her composure that long.

She'd squared her shoulders and started through the doorway when a grip closed on her elbow.

She didn't have to look to know it was Jake.

"Do you know how embarrassing this is?" he hissed, pulling her around the corner near the drinking fountain.

"Hanging around the girls' bathroom?" Sam managed. Her voice gurgled between a sob and a laugh.

"First I went to Journalism asking for you. Mr. Blair told me where you were, but some of 'em were giving me weird looks—" Jake broke off.

"Because of Rachel. Have you heard—?"

"Who hasn't?" Jake interrupted.

Sam felt as if the world tipped beneath her feet. She put a hand against the corridor wall for balance.

"And who cares?" he added.

When she didn't answer, Jake went on. "Call Sheriff Ballard and tell him not to pick you up."

"No way," Sam said. "I'm not giving up a chance to talk to him. Absolutely no way."

"I'll take you." Jake's voice was a disgusted growl.

Shocked by Jake's generosity, Sam shook her head.

Since Jake shared the truck with his brothers, he'd

endure hours of harassment if he let Sam ride along.

"Just do it," he snapped.

Sam imagined the sheriff's black-and-white off-road vehicle with the roof bar of red and amber lights pulling into the school parking lot. No one would miss seeing that.

She was about to accept Jake's offer when the bell rang and a classroom door slammed open.

The first student into the hall was Jake's loud-mouthed, baggy-panted friend Darrell.

"My *man*," Darrell howled the word as a wry compliment. He nodded at Sam in heavy-lidded approval as he approached. "I knew you'd come around," he congratulated Jake. "How *you* doin', gorgeous?"

Darrell slid a hand over his slicked-back hair and Sam thought about magic. She'd really like to vanish, right out of this hallway, forever. But if she couldn't have that, she wanted to make Darrell disappear.

In a single minute, classrooms had disgorged hundreds of curious students, and Jake's hand dropped from Sam's elbow as if he'd received an electric shock.

Jake could be a jerk, but he was her friend. Almost every mental picture she had of him involved a horse. He'd taught her to ride, to gentle, and more than that, to think like a horse. Only once, when he'd taken a terrible fall and broken his leg, had she really paid him back.

Jake always looked at ease on horseback. At

school, he was shyer and sometimes, like now, his eyes held a flicker of uncertainty.

"I'll ride with the sheriff," she told him.

Even to herself, she sounded brave. But really, she had nothing to lose. People were already talking. How much worse would it be if she had a police escort out of the parking lot?

"Okay." Jake sounded relieved. "But I'll talk to you. I want to hear what Sheriff Ballard tells you, because I have an idea of my own about Caleb and the horses."

Chapter Ten ❧

$\mathcal{T}$he sheriff's office was tucked into a corner of a new county building that housed other government offices in Darton.

On her way to the chairs arranged next to the sheriff's desk, Sam took a quick look around.

The office held high-tech radio equipment, a computer with so many cords she couldn't tell what was what, a fax machine, copy machine, and a coffeepot the size of a rain barrel.

Metal filing cabinets stood against one wall. A photograph of a large, smiling family was propped on top of one of them. The other wall held shelves of labeled boxes and an overloaded coatrack. Sam noticed a slicker, a quilted vest, waterproof overalls, a black jacket with glow-in-the-dark lettering that read "POLICE," and more.

Sinking into the blue upholstered chair facing the desk, Sam felt a surge of security, followed by surprise.

Sheriff Ballard had been watching her, with his hands folded loosely on the desk blotter. Although he needed a haircut and a mustache trim, the sheriff was alert and prepared.

"How 'bout you tell me again what happened yesterday," he encouraged her.

Sam was ready.

"I found this note in an old button box," Sam said. She unfolded the paper and handed it to him. "It's in my Mom's handwriting."

He nodded, gave the pink stationery a cursory look, then motioned Sam to go on.

"Jen and I—"

"Jennifer Kenworthy."

Sam nodded, not at all surprised he knew. "We'd planned to go looking for New Moon, a black mustang that—anyway, we rode out to Antelope Crossing instead, to see the wild horses and kind of follow up on what my mom had written."

The sheriff glanced at the note once more. In the quiet, Sam heard the emergency radio give the coded signal summoning a fire department miles away from Darton, but Sheriff Ballard just gestured for her to go on.

"I think my mom was concerned that there was antelope poaching going on and somehow it was putting the wild horses in danger."

"Pronghorn season *is* in the fall," the sheriff mused.

Sam stopped. "What do you think?"

"Go ahead and finish," he urged.

He didn't want her to get sidetracked, Sam guessed, so she explained how they had ridden into the area and seen the brown and white pronghorn grazing alongside the wild horses.

"Right away, the antelope took off. I thought they were running from us, but then the horses startled and we saw something glittering in the sagebrush—"

"Glittering?"

"Like glass or metal," Sam explained. "Really low down."

"At knee level? Ground level?" the sheriff prodded.

Sam thought for an instant. "Just above ground level. And then the horses were gone, all but the stallion, and he charged toward the sagebrush. . . ."

Sheriff Ballard looked amused, as if such dramatics over a wild stallion were to be expected from someone her age.

"He did," she insisted. "I know it's weird, but—"

"You go ahead, Samantha. Some of this pretty much matches that call we traced to Crane Crossing Mall."

What had the Sheriff said about that call last night? She tried to remember.

"Who made the call? Do you know?"

"Doesn't much matter," he said. "Probably someone being a good citizen, afraid you two would get hurt. Go ahead about the horse, though. I've been in this business long enough to know anything can happen," the Sheriff said, and Sam knew he was urging her to keep talking.

"When he charged, the guy stood up, and he had a rifle. I don't know what kind," she said, but she gave him the baggie with the shell casing inside.

Instead of looking excited, the sheriff nodded, slid the baggie to one side, and leaned forward. "Let's hear the rest."

"The guy was taking aim at the stallion and so I yelled at him and then he . . . wasn't there. I know *that* sounds weird, too, but—" Sam took a deep breath. Saying so many odd things would probably discredit her. Still, she couldn't do anything except tell the truth.

"It probably looked like that because he dropped out of sight," the sheriff said. "I know the spot you're talking about. It slants down to lower ground. All he'd have to do is back up."

"Oh, good," Sam said with a sigh.

"Did you get a look at him?" the sheriff asked.

"I tried," Sam said. "But there was nothing, like, distinctive about him. I wasn't close enough to see much, except that he looked normal. Average sized, you know?"

"And his clothes?"

"Jeans and an old brown leather jacket, I think."

For the first time, the sheriff seemed to sympathize with her frustration. "Hardest criminals to find look just like ordinary men," he said.

Sam noticed he hadn't said Caleb Sawyer was that kind of man. He didn't whip out a Wanted poster to show her, and he hadn't even taken notes.

Instead, Sheriff Ballard rose, poured himself coffee and, without asking if she wanted some, made her a cup with spoonfuls of sugar and powdered creamer.

"Now, let's see what I can help you with," he said, handing her the cup.

"Okay, what do you think of my mom's note?"

"I think, if you want to know your mom's state of mind, you need to talk with Wyatt."

State of mind? Sam squirmed in the straight-backed chair. She was probably feeling paranoid because of the stuff Rachel was saying, but that phrase sounded suspicious.

"That part about the antelope, and horses—" Sam broke off.

"Louise had a habit of driving off-road to watch wildlife." The sheriff shook his head. "I told her to be careful out there."

"Why? Was someone after her?"

The sheriff made a *halt* sign with one hand.

"That VW bus was unstable. I didn't trust its emergency handling and neither did Wyatt. A sudden swerve, for instance, could make it overturn. And probably did."

Sam imagined stampeding horses or antelope. They'd part to go around a car. But she could also imagine a driver, someone softhearted like Mom was supposed to have been, swerving instinctively, to miss them.

"I'll run a copy of this," the sheriff said, raising the note, "if you don't mind."

He took the note to the copy machine. Was he just humoring her, or did he really think it was worth investigating?

Mom, I'm doing my best, Sam thought.

Then she asked the hardest question of all. "Everyone always says my mother died instantly."

Though he had his back to her, facing the copy machine, Sam saw the sheriff's spine stiffen inside his gray uniform.

"But what does that mean? What killed her?"

The sheriff turned. "You're thirteen. I'm not saying you don't have a right to know, but I think you should ask your father."

It was too late for that, Sam thought. If Dad had wanted to tell her, he would have.

"What if you call my dad?" Sam asked.

She watched the sheriff, but it was impossible to figure out what he was thinking.

"Okay," the sheriff agreed. "I'll just step into another office and call."

He left her alone, wondering if Dad would even be home. Sam didn't see a clock in the office. There were no exterior windows to check daylight or darkness.

And cows were starting to calve on the range, making Dad's schedule unpredictable.

Sam fidgeted. If Gram answered the phone, she'd refuse to let Sheriff Ballard tell her anything. Sam's brain hated that possibility, but her heart thought it might not be so bad.

"Your dad says 'no secrets,'" Sheriff Ballard said as he reentered the office.

He squatted to open the lowest drawer on a filing cabinet, seized a folder tab, and pulled.

He slammed the drawer, then glared at the radio equipment that kept up a low-level chatter.

Was he wishing he'd get called out on an emergency?

"I don't mind saying this is uncomfortable for me," the sheriff told her, as he sat. "First, I'll tell you straight up, there were no signs of foul play. None. We all cared about Louise. If we thought someone had caused her death, we would've gone after him."

Sam felt breathless for a minute.

"What"—she felt as if something heavy compressed her chest, but she managed to get the question out—"made her die?"

He read from the folder, snapped it closed, and crossed his arms on top of it.

"The bus was upside down in a ditch running high with melted snow. It was a nice day and she had the windows rolled down. She drowned," he said bluntly. "But since she was still wearing her seat belt, she was probably unconscious."

"Drowned. No one ever said that before." Sam touched her forehead. She had the strangest falling sensation.

"You're not going to faint on me, are you?"

"I've never fainted."

But the sheriff's expression seemed to say there was always a first time. Sam didn't know how, but she pulled herself together, straightening in the chair. She cleared her throat and went on.

"Does Caleb Sawyer have a criminal record?" she asked.

"Don't worry about that," he said. "There's some minor stuff, but we're not talking murder."

"Okay," Sam said softly.

Suddenly, that was enough. In fact, it was way too much.

Sheriff Ballard went on talking. He'd investigate the possibility of antelope poaching and trespassing mustangs. BLM had federal marshals to deal with horse trouble.

"I'll go up and see Sawyer," Sheriff Ballard said. When he went on, his words took on a warning tone. "This is nothing to be taking into your own hands."

"Okay," Sam said again.

There was more that she wanted to ask, but she felt worn out from emotion.

"Your dad said Brynna would wait out front for you," the sheriff said, standing. "You go along with her, and I'll call if I uncover anything you'd find interesting."

Sam stood.

Good manners must have been stamped on her brain cells, because she remembered to shake his hand and say thank you.

"By the way," Sheriff Ballard added when she was almost to the door, "good idea, picking up the shell casing."

Sam smiled. The compliment made her feel a little better. She waved and managed to find her way down the maze of buffed hallways to the front of the office building.

Brynna's white BLM truck was parked in front of the building, engine idling. Late afternoon sun glazed the windows, so Sam couldn't see Brynna.

She hoped her stepmother wasn't in a chatty mood.

Sam's mind felt stuffed full. She wanted to go home and sleep.

But Brynna didn't even wait until Sam had climbed up into the truck to announce her bad news.

Wearing her uniform and sunglasses, Brynna looked like the cold, unemotional bureaucrat Sam had thought she was on the first day they'd met at Willow Springs.

Brynna's pale pink lips were set in a line. Her chin raised high above her perfectly pressed collar.

"The Phantom's herd has settled down on private land." Brynna kept her tone aloof and unfeeling, as if she was talking about a sudden growth of weeds.

Sam struggled for an excuse, but then Brynna added, "One way or another, they'll have to be removed."

Chapter Eleven ❧

"Whose land are the mustangs on? Caleb Sawyer's?" Sam demanded. "I want to go out there right now."

"That may be so," Brynna replied, coolly, "but it's not going to happen."

Brynna didn't deny it was the hermit's ranch, so Sam knew she'd guessed right.

"Why not? Why would you protect someone like him instead of the horses?"

"I'm not protecting him over the horses. If the horses were grazing on land he leased from BLM, it wouldn't matter. But this is his home ranch." Brynna gave a one-shouldered shrug as if she were helpless. "Under law, wild horses must stay on government land. It's my job to make sure they do."

Brynna was really going now. She didn't stop and Sam stayed silent.

"Wild horses can't go eat ranchers out of house and home. Those ranchers have a right to expect us to take the horses away."

"Away where?" Sam asked.

Brynna was speeding onto the freeway now, glancing back over her left shoulder for oncoming traffic.

"How do you think your dad would like it if mustangs were crowding our cattle?" she asked, ignoring Sam's question.

"Away *where*?" Sam demanded.

"I won't be shouted at," Brynna said, settling into driving, eyes fixed on the road ahead. Sam knew she was being punished with silence.

It wouldn't work. She'd spent hours of her life waiting out Jake Ely. And Dad. Outlasting Brynna should be a piece of cake.

Sam passed the time by staring out the window, hoping Brynna would change her mind about visiting the hermit's ranch at Snake Head Peak. Sam pictured herself facing Caleb Sawyer. She'd ask him, point-blank, if he had quarreled with her mother.

His guilt would show and she'd know if he was telling the truth.

Or, Sam sighed, feeling the longing in her chest, even if they didn't go to the ranch, if they only drove as far as Antelope Crossing, they might see the Phantom's herd.

She relived the moment when the powerful stallion had charged the shooter. He had sensed the man was a threat, but he went anyway, protecting his own.

Still staring out the window, pretending to be casual, Sam tried another strategy on her stepmother.

"Have you gone out to check for yourself that the mustangs are on his land?" Sam asked.

"They're there, Sam. You saw them. And, as far as removing the horses, well, helicopters are expensive," Brynna said, as if it were a joke. When she noticed Sam wasn't laughing, she added, "We won't do anything drastic to begin."

"To begin?"

"The mares are in foal, or have foals running alongside," Brynna said patiently. "A gather would be too stressful. We'll just try to show them it's not a peaceful place, so they'll change grazing grounds."

"What if they come back?"

"We make it unpleasant for them, Sam, and if that fails, we'll have no choice but to remove them from the range."

Then they'd have to put them up for adoption, Sam thought. She remembered a bay colt with a patch of white over one eye. She'd spotted him in the Phantom's herd around Christmas. He'd be a lively yearling by now, but he'd be terrified by the BLM's helicopter roundup and the crush of neighing horses trapped in a holding pen.

No harm to horses, Mom's note had vowed. Sam knew she and Mom were of one heart on this. She wouldn't let Brynna, the BLM, or anyone else end the Phantom's freedom. But she kept that promise to herself.

"It's not his normal territory, anyway."

"It wasn't his territory last summer," Brynna corrected. "Before that, who knows? Horses look for bunch grass. After years of drought followed by this wet winter, the growth patterns—for grass and everything else—are bound to change."

Brynna was probably right. What if the Phantom had returned his herd to a traditional grazing area? What if the Phantom's sire and grandsire had grazed there? Maybe their herd had been the one Mom had watched.

Still, Sam felt sure the man making the complaints was the one who'd sighted his rifle on the Phantom.

How could Brynna not see that?

"So, this report of trespassing horses is coming in at the same time that guy tried to shoot the Phantom. Doesn't that strike you as strange?" Sam asked.

Brynna frowned, then shook her head so hard that her red braid flipped over her shoulder.

"You're seeing coincidences because you found that note." Brynna probably didn't know she gave a faint nod. "I am taking part of that note as a reminder, though."

Sam didn't trust the way Brynna's voice had changed to a cheery lilt, so she just said, "Yeah?"

"Remember that part about shorts and sunsuits? You've grown since you got here, so you must need spring clothes. How about tomorrow, after school, we go to Crane Crossing Mall and get you a few things?"

I thought I was grounded, Sam thought.

Sam didn't remind Brynna, but she didn't rush to agree.

"Come on. Tomorrow's Friday. It's been a long week and I've been craving some pizza from Rico's, that place in the food court."

"That'd be fine," Sam decided.

"Jen could come along," Brynna offered.

"No, that's okay," Sam said.

She was mad at Jen, too. In fact, she was irritated with everyone, but she couldn't quite hold a grudge.

It was just barely possible, she supposed, that her determination was making her impatient.

She stole a quick look at Brynna and couldn't help admiring her. Intelligent and strong, already a success in an important job, she'd fallen in love with Dad and married him—and his family.

She could have picked an easier man to love. Although horses had brought Dad and Brynna together, the fate of the mustangs often pulled them apart.

Dad was a cattleman. He'd never be anything else. Brynna was a biologist, and though she classified both cattle and horses as intruders on the range, she worked to help them fit in where they could.

Sam's heart was opening just a crack, as the truck bumped across the River Bend bridge. Brynna might not be Mom, but she wasn't bad for a stepmother.

The horses in the ten-acre pasture raced along the fence when they drove into the ranch yard.

As Sam watched Buddy gallop along with the horses, she decided the calf didn't miss crossing the range with the slow-moving members of her own kind. She was happy here.

Sam climbed from the truck, feeling pretty happy herself. Then Brynna had to go and wreck it.

"Sam, be sensible," Brynna said, as she started over to see Penny. "There's no telling what your mother's list meant. And honey, you'll probably never know."

Sam considered stomping into the house to pout. Brynna was making her *that* crazy, but Dad and Dallas stood hands on hips, looking down and kicking at the dirt outside the new bunkhouse.

Their arrangement had all the earmarks of a cowboy conference, and Sam couldn't resist going to see what it was about.

Dad looked up with a welcoming expression.

"We're just talking about those yellow cows," he said, shaking his head.

"Those yellow cows" went back to Sam's childhood. Just as there'd always been a white stallion on this part of the range, there'd always been a line of Hereford cattle whose calves were born butterscotch yellow instead of brown.

The first one Sam could remember had been named Daffodil. Ranchers rarely named cattle destined for dinner tables, but this heifer had been an exception. So had her calves.

Sam remembered Daffodil had given birth to twin heifers named Petunia and Tulip, another set of twins called Iris and Poppy, and a single bull calf, Cactus. He had been sold to a rancher who'd admired him out on the range and offered to buy him.

"Buttercup's giving all the signs that she's ready to calve, but something's just not right," Dallas said.

"We've lost fewer heifers and calves since we started breeding for May calving," Dad told Sam. "The weather's better and they've eaten nutritious feed all winter, but no plan is perfect."

Sam understood Dad's frustration. Each cow was worth over a thousand dollars. Those who had healthy calves each year contributed to River Bend's well-being. When a cow died along with her unborn calf, it hurt twice as much. So it would pay to watch Buttercup carefully.

Buddy was healthy and strong. She'd probably have lots of babies, Sam thought, and she was being selfish to want to keep her as a pet.

But Dad was still talking about Buttercup.

"Where'd you see her last?" he asked.

"Out with that bunch in Bitterbrush Canyon," Dallas said. "I'm just afraid if she's not up to calving, the young one'll have trouble with coyotes."

Dad smiled to see Sam listening so intently, but only half her mind was on the yellow cow. The Phantom and his herd often took a path through Bitterbrush Canyon, up the stair-step mesas, to the tunnel that led to their secret valley.

Dallas was saying something about Ross and Pepper taking turns riding out at night, but Sam was thinking mustang mares would have to be equally careful. Newborn foals would be just as vulnerable to coyotes.

Sam reminded herself it wasn't the coyotes' fault. They were always on the prowl for food, because they had to feed the puppies waiting at home.

Just then, Blaze whined from his post at the bunkhouse door. He wagged his tail and scratched to be let in.

Although the new bunkhouse that had been built for the HARP girls was more comfortable and modern, Sam preferred this old one, built when Dad was a boy. It had a potbellied stove the cowboys still used for warmth, though they usually heated Gram's dinner contributions in a modern microwave oven.

Dallas pushed the door open for the Border collie and Sam heard Pepper practicing his harmonica. Blaze paused in the doorway, head lifted to sniff.

Dad inhaled as loudly as the dog. "That's nothing *you* whipped up," he teased Dallas.

"Crock-Pot beans and pork chops Grace left plugged in for us," Dallas admitted, then he noticed Sam watching as he rubbed the arthritis-swollen thumb of one hand. "Your gram takes good care of us during calving time."

"Did my mom used to bring you chili oil for your arthritis?" Sam asked.

"She did," Dallas said, surprised. "I haven't thought of that for a long time. No sense to it, that's what she said, but it felt kinda good, rubbing it in. How'd you come to remember that?"

"She found a list Louise made," Dad explained.

"That's nice," Dallas said. "Real nice."

But the worry in Dad's eyes reminded Sam that he hadn't talked with her since he'd given Sheriff Ballard permission to tell her everything.

Gram was serving beans and pork chops in the house, too, apologizing for a meal that had cooked all day while she planted green beans, peas, and lettuce in her garden.

"This weekend we'll make lasagna," Gram insisted. "Here, Samantha, I want you to read this and start letting it settle into your mind."

Sam took the index card. It had a red spatter on one corner. Lasagna sauce, she guessed. It was her mother's recipe, written in her mother's handwriting.

Serves ??? it said at the bottom, reminding Sam of the question marks Mom had drawn as she wrote out her list, wondering if Caleb Sawyer had a criminal record.

"Not that much to it, is there?" Brynna asked, glancing over Sam's shoulder.

"No," Sam admitted. With its list of ingredients followed by assembly and cooking directions, it looked pretty simple, but Brynna's comment still annoyed her.

"I've found it helps to read the recipe over before you make it," Gram said.

"She'll have plenty of time to do that and have it ready when we get home from the range Saturday night," Dad said.

Sam felt her eyes widen. Dad had been acting nice tonight. Nicer than normal, even. So, he couldn't mean what she thought he did.

"You all are riding out . . . ?" Sam began.

"We're going to need everyone spread out across the cows' usual territory, making sure calving is going fine. Your gram wasn't planning to go, but I asked her to take your place." Dad glanced down at his hands. "Now, I'm going upstairs to wash up. You do the same and help your gram get dinner on the table."

Moving like a sleepwalker, Sam crossed to the kitchen sink and used the bar of white soap Gram kept there. She rubbed her palms together for a long time.

"He doesn't want you to make a habit of doing dangerous things and keeping them from us," Gram said, handing Sam a clean towel.

"I know," Sam said, but she was angry all over again.

It wasn't fair. Everyone else would ride out in the cool May morning with saddlebags full of lunch. They'd stay on horseback all day long, checking hills and canyons, gulches and streamside pastures for cows and their babies. All day, they'd have the sun on their cheeks and the wind in their hair.

She'd be left at home, and she'd done nothing wrong. She'd neglected to tell Dad something, but that wasn't the same as actually *doing* something wrong.

Sam stared at the recipe card sitting on the kitchen counter. Her mother had drawn an asterisk and written a footnote that said: "Chill knife thoroughly before chopping onions. Prevents tears!!!"

Thanks, Mom, Sam thought as she hung the towel back over its rack, *but I'll be crying over more than onions.*

Chapter Twelve ⌐

*A*fter dinner, Brynna helped Gram with the dishes while Dad took Sam into the living room. He turned on a lamp, but not the television, and asked Sam to sit down on the couch.

Weak from all the trouble she was in, Sam sank into the couch cushions, on top of a book.

Sam pulled it out from under herself. The thick scrapbook was covered in gold brocade. It looked vaguely familiar, but she didn't recognize it until she turned it over. The lettering on the front said, "Our Wedding."

"Oh," Sam said. She felt strange holding it. "I haven't seen this in a long time."

"It's been put away," Dad said as he settled beside

her. "I've been thinking, though, since you heard about the end of it all from Sheriff Ballard, you might like to see how our life together began."

Sam's eyes filled with tears, but she refused to let them fall. When Dad put it that way, Mom's life sounded so short. For a moment her hands stroked the book's cover, and then she looked inside.

The scrapbook was as energetic and disorganized as everything else of her mother's. The first snapshots showed Mom before the wedding. Her hair looked perfectly styled. Glossy and woven with daisies, it fell in red waves to her elbows. Mom wore jeans. She was eating a sandwich and talking on the phone while she held out a placating hand to a very young Aunt Sue. Dressed in a long, pink gown, Mom's sister must have been telling Mom to hurry. Gram stood beside them both, in a full-skirted blue dress, grinning.

"Mom looks like a hippie," Sam said.

"I guess she was, in a way," Dad replied.

The only formal photograph covered an entire page. It showed the wedding ceremony itself, inside the Darton Methodist Church. Mom and Dad faced each other, holding hands. Sam couldn't see their expressions, and probably no one else had, either. They were pledging to love each other forever, so why should they look at anyone else?

Sam sniffed and blinked, telling herself the photograph only looked blurry because of the multicolored sunlight streaming down on them from stained-glass windows.

A copy of the wedding invitation, a pressed daisy, and a silver-edged pink napkin bearing a lipsticked mouth print were stuck haphazardly under the plastic of the next page. A tiny slip of paper—half of one, really—that might have been from a fortune cookie, read, "and then there was you."

Sam glanced up to see if Dad was ready for her to turn the page, but he was staring off, not looking at her or the album.

More pictures had been taken here at the ranch. Mom's lacy white peasant dress matched Aunt Sue's pink one, but while Mom was laughing in every picture, Aunt Sue seemed uncomfortable. Here, she adjusted the wreath of wild flowers on her hair. There, she frowned at the big dogs gamboling in Mom's wake.

Sam recognized Jake's parents, dancing together even though each held a wriggling toddler. And there was Helen Coley, who worked at the Slocum house now. But in this picture, she wore a spring-green pantsuit and rolled her eyes in delight over something she'd just eaten from a buffet plate. Lila and Jed Kenworthy stood shoulder to shoulder clapping, whether to music or Mom's antics, Sam couldn't tell.

Even though the pictures had been taken fifteen years before, Dad didn't look much different than he did now. His smile had been a little broader, without the lines that bracketed it now. But he looked like what he was, a cowboy, and in every picture he was touching Mom.

No, Sam thought, as she checked each page, it was more like Dad was reaching for her, trying to keep in touch as she stood on her toes fixing a bell-shaped decoration, or squatted to talk with a toddler. He reached up for the reins as Mom, skirt hiked up and bare feet dangling, sat astride a spirited, half-rearing Sweetheart.

Even in the last picture, where they were dancing, Mom had twirled out to the end of Dad's arm. Her head was thrown back with giggles and the hem of her skirt was held up with one hand. The fingertips of the other hand were outstretched, just missing Dad's grasp.

"It shows, doesn't it?" Dad studied the photo. "I could never really hold on to her."

"Sheriff Ballard said her VW bus was unstable," Sam began.

"It was, and she knew it." Dad's hands closed into fists, until he met Sam's eyes. "Anytime she went somewhere with you, though, she took the Buick and strapped you into one of those baby car seats."

"Why did you let her drive it?" Sam heard her own beseeching tone.

"Sam, I've asked myself that a million times. Truth is, there was no telling Louise what to do and what not to do. She knew her own mind." Dad wore a lopsided smile as he added, "And sometimes, she just plain let her feelings run away with her."

"Or maybe she was thinking about something else. Like Caleb Sawyer," Sam said. "Why did she put that stuff on her list?"

"I've been thinking on that, and it's like I said before. She had some idea he was hurting wild horses to keep them off his land."

"Do you think he was?"

"I don't know," Dad said. "Caleb's always been a loner. Rumor says he was a mustanger in the old days. Maybe that kind of talk got her going. And since his is just a little cow-calf operation, everyone's always wondered how he pays the taxes on that ranch, and where he gets his money."

Money. Sam sat up straighter. One name came to her mind: Linc Slocum.

And hadn't Brynna said Caleb used Slocum's name every time he called BLM to get the horses off his land? What were those two planning? Someone needed to question them both.

"Sam." Brynna's tone was apologetic as she stuck her head into the living room. "I'm sorry to interrupt, but Jen's on the phone. Grace said she called earlier, too."

In the minute that Sam hesitated, deciding just how mad she was at Jen, she noticed Brynna's expression. Not since the first days after the honeymoon had Sam seen Brynna look so unsure.

Brynna's blue eyes flicked from Dad to Sam and back again. She cared about them both, and the horses, but then there was Mom, Dad's first love. Sam didn't enjoy Brynna's suffering, but she wasn't about to stop following the clues left in Mom's note.

"We're done here," Dad said, rising.

"I'll talk with Jen," Sam said.

As she started for the kitchen, Sam heard Dad talking behind her.

"We've still got some daylight left. How 'bout going for a ride? It'll help Penny settle in and I'll work some of the orneriness out of Strawberry."

"Oh," Sam said, turning, "I forgot to tell you." She hesitated, seeing Dad's arm around Brynna's shoulders. "Strawberry *has* been mean to Penny." It seemed sort of useless to mention it now, but Sam added, "I saw her this morning."

"Thanks," Brynna said, "I knew I could count on you to help with her."

Sam felt a little guilty as she picked up the telephone receiver from the kitchen counter.

"Hello?" she said, but heard only dial tone. Sam hung up the phone. "I guess she got tired of waiting."

"Call her back," Gram said.

Sam's hand was still on the receiver when the phone rang again. This time it was Jake.

"Hi," she said in surprise. Sure, Jake had said he would call, but he rarely did. Face-to-face communication was tough enough for him. On the phone, she had to imagine half of what he intended to say. "Did you call to tell me your idea about the horses?"

"Not mine, really."

"Then whose?"

"Dad and Grandfather."

Jake's grandfather, MacArthur Ely, was an elder in the Shoshone tribe, and he'd lived here all his life. If *he* was suspicious of Caleb Sawyer, there was definitely something to be suspicious about.

"Okay," Sam said, making her tone encouraging. As she waited, Dad and Brynna passed through the kitchen. "What did they say?"

"Shan Stonerow and Sawyer used to be partners."

Sam's pulse sped up. She'd never met either man, but Shan Stonerow was rumored to be a rough and unscrupulous horse tamer. "Quick and dirty" was the way Mac, Jake's grandfather, had described Stonerow's way of training unbroken horses.

"What did they do to the horses?" Sam asked.

"Don't know for sure, but they took out-of-state hunters after pronghorn during calving season."

"I thought baby pronghorn were called fawns."

"They are," Jake said.

"And Sheriff Ballard said pronghorn season was in the fall."

"It is. You gonna let me talk?"

Sam wanted to snap that she'd been dragging every word out of him. But she didn't.

Instead, she said, "Go ahead, Jake. Sorry."

"I mean, while most ranchers were tending their stock, they made a fortune with illegal hunts."

Sam's imagination filled in the details, picturing the brown and white pronghorn. They were incredibly fast and they could jump over every rock or clump of sagebrush, but some might still be pregnant in spring. Others would be slowed by newborns. They'd be easier targets than usual, local ranchers would be distracted by calving, so they wouldn't notice the poaching, and the horses would just be in the way.

It would be simple for dishonest men to charge lots of money for a guaranteed trophy, and never get caught.

Except by Mom.

"I've got to tell Sheriff Ballard."

"One problem," Jake said.

"Don't look for a way to stop me, Jake Ely."

"Be sensible for once," Jake said.

Sam almost exploded. Twice tonight she'd been ordered to be sensible. As far as she could tell, she was the only one who was! How sensible were Brynna and Jake being, ignoring a crime taking place right under their noses?

". . . all hearsay," Jake was going on. "It's probably true, but it was a long time ago. . . ."

"I bet he's still doing it," Sam insisted. "I saw him try to shoot the Phantom!"

"No witnesses. No evidence."

"*I'm* a witness!" she growled. "And I gave Sheriff Ballard some evidence."

The sheriff hadn't been excited by her testimony or Mom's note. If he had, he would have marched out and arrested Caleb Sawyer.

She hated it, but the sheriff had to go by what he could prove. Then, all at once, she knew what to do.

"I'll tell Brynna!" Sam shouted.

"That pierced my eardrum," Jake complained.

"Okay, but don't you think that's what I should do? She has the power of the federal government behind her, right? The horses are under government protection, so people can't go around shooting them, or even *at* them. Besides—"

"Take a breath, Brat."

"—she knows a bunch of Division of Wildlife guys and they could handle the poaching part of it and put Sawyer away!"

"Maybe." Jake sounded unconvinced. "But it's been a long time."

"If he's gotten away with it for a long time, wouldn't arresting him be even more"—Sam fumbled for a word—"urgent?"

"Maybe," Jake repeated.

Sam glanced around the kitchen. Gram had left.

Just the same, Sam whispered as she said, "Well, if *they* don't do anything about it—"

"Don't say it," Jake interrupted. "Don't even say

something as stupid and pigheaded as that. You're already grounded. Do you want them to send you back to San Francisco?"

"What?"

"I said, be smart, Samantha."

"That's not what you said." Sam swallowed. Jake had been gone when Dad said she'd been safer in San Francisco. "Who told you my dad—?"

"Nobody," Jake said. He let the word fall like a rock.

But somehow he'd known. Sam drew a deep breath.

In her mind, she looked from Aunt Sue's bay window and saw nothing but fog spangled with streetlights.

Nothing could be worse than being sent away from the ranch and Ace and the Phantom, but that would sure make life easier for Brynna and Dad and Gram, since they all wanted her out of harm's way.

The cowboys could take over her chores and Brynna could hire Jake and Jen to work with the HARP girls. Sam wondered if she'd be missed at all.

"I haven't heard anything," Jake insisted. "That was just a 'what if.'"

"Maybe," Sam said, giving him a taste of his own brevity.

"Look, do you want a ride in to school tomorrow?" Jake asked. "I don't trust you to get there on your own."

Where did he think she was going to go? And then she knew. Jake thought she'd go face Caleb Sawyer herself.

"I'll get there," Sam said. "But first I need to talk with Jen. She owes me a big favor, and I've just figured out how she can pay me back."

Chapter Thirteen ॐ

Sam didn't know whether it was excitement or fear that kept her from eating the next morning.

Her mind had assembled, scattered, and reassembled jigsaw puzzle pieces of information all night long.

The homemade cinnamon rolls had smelled so good that she'd given in to Gram's urging to take one, carefully wrapped, in her backpack, but she wasn't sure she'd be able to swallow it.

Gram had just paused to let her off at the bus stop and Sam had barely opened the Buick door when Jen, wearing new pink corduroy pants and a short-sleeved fuchsia turtleneck, descended on Sam.

"I'm sorry, I'm sorry. Don't be mad at me," Jen said, pulling Sam by the arm when she drew back.

"As a good friend, I know I owe you a crazy spell after the way I was acting when my parents were messed up!"

Jen wouldn't let Sam escape. She wrapped her in a hug.

"And I know that this is a much bigger deal than the stuff with Golden Rose because it's your mom. So just don't say anything."

"Can I breathe, if I promise not to say anything?"

"I guess," Jen said. "And actually, you're allowed to talk, if you promise not to yell at me."

"I won't yell, but I have a question and a favor to ask," Sam said.

She told Jen about Jake's theory and noticed her friend was nodding.

"Oh, and here's the best part. I think someone's trying to keep us away from there. Someone called the sheriff and reported us!"

"What do you mean?" Jen asked.

"That afternoon when we saw the guy with the gun? Someone called the sheriff anonymously from Crane Crossing Mall—"

"He traced the call?" Jen's voice was faint.

"—and reported . . ." Sam's voice trailed off as Jen's face turned milky and her eyes grew round behind her glasses.

"It was me," Jen confessed. "I didn't want whoever it was to get away with it, and I was afraid, with the stuff Rachel was saying about you, well, they wouldn't take you seriously, but am I in trouble?"

It was Sam's turn to hug Jen. Her best friend had tried to protect her, even though she knew it might get her in trouble.

"He doesn't care who it was," Sam said once she'd released Jen. "He said it wasn't important, just someone being a good citizen."

"He's right," Jen said. Then, after she'd caught her breath, Jen agreed the pronghorn-poaching scheme sounded just like something Linc Slocum would be involved in.

"It's just his kind of skullduggery, but he wasn't around back then. He didn't come to Nevada until about two years ago."

"I thought of that," Sam said. "But —"

"But it's exactly his kind of creepy, money-making scheme," Jen agreed. Then she looked faintly confused. "Hey, do you have something delicious in your backpack, or is that new perfume?"

"Not perfume," Sam said, brushing her friend's curiosity aside. "But listen, I told Brynna about Jake's theory, and she says if Sawyer was leading illegal hunts on public lands or harming mustangs, he's dead meat."

"She said that?" Jen gasped.

"Not exactly," Sam admitted, "but she had that look in her eye."

Jen didn't speak. Instead, she very pointedly stuck out her tongue and pretended to bite it.

Sam smiled. Jen was trying not to lecture Sam about Brynna's value as a stepmother again.

"You don't have to tell me. I know Dad could have married a person who was a lot worse," Sam said.

"So are you going to get her a Mother's Day present?" Jen asked.

"I don't know. Sometimes I feel like I should, and other times it seems sort of disloyal," Sam said.

Jen nodded just as the yellow school bus roared into view. Once they were seated in their usual bench, she asked, "So where does the favor come in?"

"I want to go see Caleb Sawyer."

"I won't bother listing everything that's wrong with that idea. You probably already know, right? Starting with the whole guns and grounding thing, progressing through bodily harm and not talking to strangers."

"I know. But I've figured out how to do it safely. And that's where you come in." Sam paused, then frowned as Jen stopped twirling the end of her braid and actually nibbled on it. "I've never seen you do that before."

"Do what?"

"Uh, eat the tassel on your braid?"

"Yikes," Jen tossed the braid away as if it were a snake. "That's because I haven't done it since I was about ten. My parents finally bribed me to stop—with a way-too-expensive chemistry set. I only do it when I'm facing extreme stress. So tell me, Sam. What do you want me to do?"

"Did Ryan pick you up after school yesterday?"

"Yeah," Jen said cautiously. "And he actually took me to Clara's for a Coke before he drove me home! Why?"

Sam sighed in satisfaction. It meant missing a trip to the mall with Brynna, but who cared?

"Would I let anything bad happen to my best friend?" Sam tried to sound soothing.

"Probably not," Jen said.

Sam thought of a way to seal their truce. She pulled her backpack into her lap, opened it, and took out a waxed paper-wrapped lump.

"I can't bribe you with anything as exciting as a chemistry set, but I can offer you half of this cinnamon roll."

Jen inhaled deeply, then sighed. "You can count on me to do whatever you've got in mind, but it's really sad that it only took food to convince me."

The first half of the school day went smoothly. As far as Sam could tell, no one peeped over a book to get a look at a crazy person. Her.

It was Friday and, amid the usual chatter about weekend parties and movies, Sam heard complaints about Mother's Day, which was bound to get in the way of fun with friends.

As she listened, Sam felt a cold hollow beneath

her breastbone. She wanted to speak up, to remind the whiners that their mothers would be gone, someday. But she didn't. Someday was too far away. She probably couldn't convince them it would ever come.

She and Jen split a sandwich and sipped chocolate milk shakes as they finalized their after-school plan. Jen stood by, fidgeting, as Sam used a pay phone to call Brynna and tell her she had an assignment for Journalism, which meant they'd have to delay their trip to the mall.

"That's a shame, but we'll do it in the next few days," Brynna had said. "Your classes are top priority."

Feeling guilty, Sam slipped into Journalism early, still sipping her milk shake. Mr. Blair was pretty cool about allowing food in class, as long as no one made a mess. Sam glanced around for Rachel. She hadn't seen her all day, even in the P.E. class they shared.

Mr. Blair and RJay were the only ones in the Journalism room. The emptiness was a relief.

Sam crossed to the assignment clipboard hanging on the wall. Mr. Blair wanted a photo story on old Nevada.

Sam nodded. If she signed up for it, she could convince herself she hadn't lied to Brynna.

What could be more photogenic than shots of the high desert cabin of the hermit of Snake Head Peak?

As Sam signed her name next to the story, she noticed Mr. Blair motioning her up to his desk. RJay stood nearby. Was this the "think fast" moment RJay had alerted her to yesterday?

Sam walked toward them, trying to look confident.

She held her breath, wondering if this was about the editorship. Mr. Blair wouldn't keep her in suspense. He always got right to the point.

"So here's the thing, Forster," he said. "I'm impressed with your photography, but you're not showing me much in terms of people skills."

"Management skills, more," RJay corrected.

Stalling for time, Sam sipped her milk shake. Yuck. It was goopy and no longer cold.

"I'm just a reporter. I don't get a chance to boss anyone," Sam protested.

The bell to begin class rang and more than a few students let their eyes wander to the meeting at the teacher's desk.

Mr. Blair smiled as if Sam had said exactly what he'd wanted her to say. "RJay, let her take charge of assigning stories for this issue. That'll show what kind of bossing skills she has.

"Forster, that clipboard lists every story, but precious few reporters have claimed 'em. Thirty minutes from now, I want you back at this desk to show me who's doing what. Got it?"

Sam and RJay nodded.

"Go," said Mr. Blair, and turned back to his computer.

Sam took the clipboard from its wall hook and held it with trembling hands.

This was just great. It wasn't bad enough that she'd made a fool of herself in class and been accused of brain damage. Now Mr. Blair had given her a job guaranteed to make everyone hate her, too.

Oh well, at least it would keep her mind off the awful chance that she'd get caught today. But she wouldn't think about that now. She had to be brave. And fast. They couldn't send her away to San Francisco if she uncovered the truth about Caleb Sawyer.

Sam refocused on the clipboard and started moving around class with it. Surprisingly, once she explained what she was doing, no one resisted.

"Give me some sports stuff," said a guy named Zeke. "My grade in here could use some CPR. And I've got the computer until the end of the period," he announced to the room in general.

"Fine," Sam said. Next, she managed to push prom coverage off on underclassmen who didn't have the excuse of getting their hair done or renting tuxes, because the dance was restricted to juniors and seniors.

She found someone willing to cover the school play in exchange for two free tickets and extra credit in English.

Finally, Sam sat biting her lip, studying the three remaining stories. She glanced up at the clock, only to see Rachel approaching.

Tailored and crisp, the aqua shirtdress Rachel wore was almost businesslike, except for its length. As Rachel approached with the menacing prowl of a tigress, her arms stayed close to her sides. Her skirt hem rode high on her thighs, way above her fingertips.

Just as she had all year long, Sam fumed at the unfairness. If *she'd* worn that dress, some school administrator would have sent her home to change. Even if Rachel looked great, shouldn't she be reprimanded for breaking the dress code?

But Rachel stood before her, waiting, as if she actually wanted to claim an assignment.

Then, she tapped an iridescent, taffy-colored fingernail on the list of stories.

"I'll do the interview with Jake Ely," Rachel offered.

Of course you will, Sam thought, *just to make me mad*. But after two or three seconds, Sam grinned.

Jake had won his long-distance event in every track meet so far. He'd definitely go to regionals and maybe compete for Darton High on the state level. The *Dialogue* needed an interview with him, but everyone who knew Jake also knew it would be impossible to make him discuss his winning season.

Jake was too modest. But Rachel wasn't familiar with that concept.

"You're on," Sam said, scrawling Rachel's name next to the story.

Suddenly, the rich girl looked wary.

"Unless you want to do it," Rachel said.

"No, go for it," Sam urged. Then, when she saw Rachel's easy victory was making her increasingly suspicious, Sam added, "I wonder if you could do one more thing, a little piece on Kris's pitching for the baseball team? He's having a pretty good season, too. And I was hoping he'd have time to talk with you for the paper."

Kris Cameron was Rachel's handsome, broad-shouldered boyfriend. Undeniably the cutest guy at Darton High, he was not only quarterback on the football team, but pitcher for the baseball team as well.

"But if you think he'd be too busy . . ." Sam said, shrugging.

"Too busy for me? You must be joking," Rachel trilled. "He'll make time. Kris would do anything for me."

"Ah well, who wouldn't?" RJay asked sarcastically as Rachel went slinking away. Then he tilted his head to look at the clipboard. "Two stories and"—he glanced up at the clock—"five minutes left. Lookin' good, Sam, keep going."

Sam scanned the classroom in time to see Cammy edging toward the door. Time to make her getaway and buy Queen Rachel's diet Coke from the machine in the faculty room.

"Cammy!" Sam shouted. When the ringleted blonde jumped, Sam beckoned her over. "I had to save you from yourself."

"Huh?" Cammy asked.

"Never mind," Sam told her. "I need you to do two stories for this issue. One is on the campus cleanup campaign."

"That won't be fun," Cammy complained.

"But the other one is," Sam said hurriedly. She was out of time. She could feel Mr. Blair's eyes boring into her back and see Rachel eavesdropping from her desk. "You get to do 'Heard in the Halls,' you know, where you just listen for interesting or weird snippets of conversations."

"Oh, I can do that," Cammy said. Her ringlets bounced as she nodded. "Sign me up."

Sam strode over to Mr. Blair and presented the clipboard with a victorious flourish.

He gave the names a cursory glance.

"Great," he said, "now take a bunch of dynamite photos for that piece on old Nevada, get a few interviews"—he reached into a bottom drawer for a miniature tape recorder and slapped it into her hand—"and make sure this doesn't stall out on you. It's been known to do that. In short, just work hard and keep your nose clean till the end of the year and you're the new photo editor."

Sam tried to maintain a mature manner. It lasted until she'd slipped the tape recorder into her backpack and checked out a class camera. Then, she couldn't stand it. She crowed in delight and spun around to give RJay a high five. And really, she didn't care if she looked crazy. She was just acting like a freshman.

"Forster, get rid of that milk shake before you spill it," Mr. Blair growled.

Laughing, Sam headed toward the classroom trash can.

Rachel moved in the same direction, with sly certainty, as if she had something planned. She held a balled-up piece of notebook paper as if it were a stage prop.

"Cammy," Rachel purred as she passed the girl's desk. "I have a Heard in the Halls item for you."

Sam gritted her teeth. It was just like Rachel to fabricate something, when the point was to assemble little bits of overheard conversation.

In a loud whisper, Rachel said, "S. F. is crazy, and not in a fun way!"

There was no doubt who S. F. was, Sam thought as Cammy dutifully scribbled down Rachel's words. Sam felt a red-hot blush consume her excitement over the editorship.

Rachel strolled on as if she'd done nothing. If they both kept walking, Sam thought, they'd reach the same place at the same time. She couldn't let Rachel stage another sideshow, so she tossed her half-finished milk shake toward the can and turned back toward her desk.

Rachel's shriek made Sam look in time to see a splash of milk shake fanning through the air.

If it had happened in slow motion, Sam couldn't have seen it more clearly. A glob of chocolate split into droplets and they were homing in on Rachel's aqua dress.

"Look what she did!" Rachel yelled. She whirled toward Mr. Blair, pointing to the chocolate spatters on her dress. "She did it on purpose!"

Slowly, Mr. Blair looked up from the paperwork spread on his desk.

"Simmer down, Slocum. Just run down to the rest room and clean yourself up."

"Clean myself up?" Rachel screamed. "This cannot be fixed in a rest room. You can't possibly have any idea what this dress cost!"

"I'm sure she'd be glad to tell us." The remark came from somewhere behind Sam, but she didn't dare turn to see who'd said it.

It was a good thing she didn't.

"What about her?" Rachel lunged forward in a wave of strong perfume. She raked her fingernail like a claw at Sam's nose, but missed as Sam drew back. "I want her punished."

Mr. Blair had finally pushed his papers aside. Anyone paying attention could have seen he'd had about enough of Rachel's dramatics.

"It was an accident," Sam began.

Mr. Blair nodded in agreement.

"It wasn't!" Rachel screeched. Enraged, she shoved a desk. It hit another desk, which tipped over, colliding with Cammy's. The ringleted girl jumped up and backed away with round eyes.

"That's enough," Mr. Blair said.

"How can you believe it was an accident? She's crazy! And I'm going home!" Rachel tried to kick a desk out of her way, and missed. She shrieked in rage, and kicked again. This time her high-heeled shoe flew off. It somersaulted through the air to titters of laughter.

"This is not fair!" Rachel grappled the shoe from the floor and jammed her foot inside, then stood trembling, fists pumped in short bursts at her sides. "She hates me because I'm everything she's not!"

No one spoke up to agree with her.

"Right?" Rachel scanned the amazed faces around her.

Still no one spoke. The only sound was Zeke, tapping away at the computer keyboard.

"Oh, forget this," Rachel snapped in disgust. "I've had enough of you people."

As if nothing of consequence were going on, Mr. Blair had gone back to his reading. He didn't glance up when he said, "That'll count as cutting class, but suit yourself."

"I will!" Rachel said. She flounced from the room, slipping just a little in the puddle of chocolate goop in the doorway.

"Forster, clean up that mess before the bell rings," Mr. Blair said.

Sam rushed to do it, but as Rachel's shoes echoed in the hall and the corridor door slammed, Sam noticed no one asked her if she *had* done it on purpose. In fact, over the tapping of the computer keys, she heard Zeke comment, "Now *that's* what I call crazy."

Chapter Fourteen ❧

"*T*his is rather exciting!"

Ryan Slocum grinned and tightened his grip on the steering wheel of his father's champagne-colored Jeep Cherokee. Sam cradled the school's expensive camera on her lap. And Snake Head Peak towered up on the horizon.

Sam had a feeling everything was going to be fine. As she'd left class, details of Rachel's tantrum were already being broadcast in the halls. No one was gossiping about crazy Sam Forster.

And she was going to be photo editor next year. She felt proud, but should she race home and announce her good news tonight? Or should she save it, in case she needed to prove she was too good a kid to be sent back to San Francisco?

Sam's mind was jerked back to the job before her as the Cherokee bucked over hardened ruts that had once been the mud surrounding Aspen Creek. The ride was rougher than on horseback, but smoother than Jake's truck.

At least on this third visit to Antelope Crossing, Sam knew they were headed the right way.

"You're not certain exactly where the cottage is, though," Ryan said. "Is that correct?"

"I sort of know," Sam said, but Ryan actually looked cheery about getting lost in the wild West.

Sam couldn't help contrasting Ryan with his sister. Sure, Rachel's England-reared brother had the same lean build and coffee-brown hair, and he dressed with more care than the usual Darton schoolboy. Right now, for instance, he actually wore cuff links with his open-necked shirt.

Unlike his sister, Ryan loved horses. He'd competed on heavy hunters, won two English dressage titles, and helped Sam reveal that Tinkerbell, a horse slated for slaughter, was a talented jumper. Challenged by Jake's plan to ride a wild Indian pony in the Superbowl of Horsemanship, Ryan had gentled a gelding from the Blind Faith Mustang Sanctuary and ridden him in the race.

Best of all, Ryan hadn't asked *why* when Jen had told him to bring his father's new Cherokee and to be prepared for cross-country travel.

If Ryan planned to be Jen's boyfriend—and that

still wasn't a sure thing—spontaneity would be an asset. She and Jen enjoyed life's sudden twists and turns.

Not everyone did. Jake Ely, for instance, Sam thought. While he might do crazy things on his own, he'd never have driven her to Caleb Sawyer's wilderness cabin. Last night, he wouldn't even let her talk about it.

And twice today, at school, he'd touched his head and raised his eyebrows, asking silently how her head was from bumping his truck window the other night. Where she was concerned, Jake was just too careful.

"Thanks again for the ride," Sam told Ryan, appreciating him all the more. "I need this photo essay to get a good grade in Journalism, and I think the light's going to be just perfect."

Jen gave a disbelieving snort. She knew the story was mostly camouflage for her real reason for coming out here. But Ryan didn't seem to notice.

"You're completely welcome," he said, then glanced through the windshield and up. "Those dramatic clouds should photograph nicely, though it feels as if we're in for a bit of a blow."

"Wait," Sam said, suddenly. "The horses—where did they all go?"

Ryan braked and stopped.

The Cherokee shivered as a blast of wind hit it broadside. Antelope Crossing, where pronghorn and horses had grazed just two days ago, was an empty expanse of sage and sand.

"It's earlier," Jen said. "Last time we were here, it was almost dusk. That's a safer time for both herds. Maybe we'll see them on our way out."

"Maybe," Sam answered. She tried to believe the overcast sky and rising wind had fooled her.

Ryan drove on. As a dilapidated wooden cabin came into sight up ahead, she was glad it wasn't night. The man inside that cabin had been her mother's enemy.

"What a striking rock formation," Ryan commented. "The low outcroppings on each side make it a natural fortress, don't you think?"

Sam glanced up. Ryan was right. From that crown of rocks above the cabin, you could hide out and look down on any visitors.

The peak cast a black shadow and they'd just moved into it, but Sam thought only of the barking dog chained beside the porch of the old cabin.

Her worry disappeared as she realized the dog, which seemed to be mostly Labrador, hadn't even stood up. He was only barking out of duty.

"You can let me out here and I'll walk up," Sam told Ryan.

"It might be a good idea to sound the horn, first," Jen advised him.

"Whatever for?" Ryan asked.

"Caleb Sawyer won't recognize your truck, and

since we know he has a rifle . . ."

"So many people out here do." Ryan sounded puzzled.

"Yeah, and Dad says some of these old desert rats shoot first and ask what the heck you want, later."

When Ryan honked, the dog turned more serious. It lurched to its feet and barked louder as a door creaked in the wind.

Sam draped the camera strap around her neck and patted the pocket where she'd stashed Mr. Blair's mini tape recorder. She should have practiced with it on the way here, but now there was no time.

Sam reached for the truck door.

She'd go before she lost her nerve. *Now*. But her hand hesitated on the door as a slow-moving figure appeared on the porch.

"No rifle," Jen said, sighing.

"And with *that* heartening farewell, I'm out of here," Sam said.

She shoved open the door and slammed it behind her. She wanted to announce to Caleb Sawyer that she wasn't sneaking up on him.

She'd only taken a few steps when Jen lowered the truck window.

"Psst," Jen hissed. "Keep him outside to talk and take lots of pictures while you ask him stuff. That way he won't feel cornered. You don't want him to be stressed."

Sam gave her friend a quelling look.

"And keep checking the tape to make sure it's turning. This is probably your only chance to build a body of evidence."

Why couldn't Jen have offered advice when they were still inside the truck, out of Caleb Sawyer's hearing? Still, "body of evidence" had a nice official ring to it. Sam squared her shoulders and walked.

Wind brought the smell of dog, cooking, and mildew. Sam looked at the battered tents gathered to one side of the cabin and wondered why they were there.

She was just wishing for a sweatshirt to pull on over her blue shirt when the man on the porch called out.

"Hey! Get outta here!"

"I'm Samantha Forster from Darton High School and—"

"Whattya want?"

So much for introductions, Sam thought. She reached into her pocket and pushed the start button on the tape recorder.

"I'm doing a story—"

"You're that kid with the bay horse, ain't ya?" he said, and gestured toward the range where he'd shot at the Phantom. "What're you doin' drivin' Slocum's truck?"

Chills rained over her. The gooseflesh on her arms wasn't caused by the spring wind.

He knew Linc Slocum. He must have seen him

recently, too. Linc had gotten this truck just months ago, when he was hunting cougars.

Slocum and Sawyer were up to no good. She just knew it. Still, she tried to act calm.

"I'm not driving the truck, sir. Mr. Slocum's son, Ryan, brought me over to talk with you."

Caleb Sawyer gave no sign he'd heard. Maybe the dog's barking had drowned out her voice. Maybe he was studying her as intently as she was him.

Caleb Sawyer's face wore a lifelong tan from working outdoors. Wrinkles around his eyes and mouth looked as if they'd been tightened with drawstrings.

Dressed in a flannel shirt rubbed thin as pajamas, and brown trousers, he shuffled along in boots bleached by alkali dust. His frizzled hair showed a mix of brown and gray and it hadn't been cut in so long, he had to push it away from his eyes. Then he squinted as if Sam stood in full sunlight, instead of shadows.

"Jet!" he shouted, waving at the dog. It sat in silence, instantly.

"What did you say?" he asked.

"Linc Slocum's son, Ryan, brought me out here to talk with you," Sam repeated. "I'm doing a story about old Nevada for the school newspaper."

Caleb Sawyer's head tilted to one side. Maybe he didn't like being part of "old" Nevada.

"What about Slocum's car?" he asked, again, and suddenly Sam realized he was hard of hearing.

She moved closer and talked more loudly.

"*Ryan* Slocum drove me here."

"The boy," Caleb said, nodding.

Something wet made Sam gasp. She turned to find the gray-muzzled dog nudging her hand out of its clenched fist. She rubbed Jet's sleek black head. It wasn't the dog's fault he had an evil master.

"Ain't good for much anymore. Chases skunks, is why he's chained up."

"Our dog chases porcupines," Sam said, before she thought better of sympathizing.

"Whose dog?" Sawyer scowled, still trying to make sense of her presence. "Who are you?"

Sam thought better of telling him her last name. If he knew Brynna, he'd know she worked for the BLM and he'd probably refuse to talk. If he knew Dad, he'd know Wyatt Forster took care of the land and didn't approve of poaching. If Sawyer remembered Mom . . .

Sam decided not to take a chance.

"I'm a student at Darton High," she said, then lifted the camera. "Can I take a picture of Jet?"

"Don't know why you would," he said, rubbing the dog's ears. "Good for nothin' old cur, but go on."

She stared through the eyepiece, snapping pictures. She should ask her big questions, now, while he was pleased by her appreciation of Jet.

"I heard you could tell me about mustanging in the old days."

Caleb's head jerked up. "That was never nothin'

but a side job and legal in them days."

Mustanging hadn't been legal for over thirty years, but Sam didn't say so.

"I'm a huntin' guide, best in the county. I want in on that bison thing of his." Sawyer nodded toward Linc Slocum's truck. "I could take hunters out to find them big woolly critters. Antelope are harder than deer, and those mustangs?" he shook his head in grudging respect. "They'll take you to where the trail ends, and just when you think they're cornered, you'll be all alone. Hardest critter to catch, even with water traps, snares, creasing . . ."

The old man lowered himself to sit on the porch step, then stared off into his memories, but any sympathy Sam had felt for him vanished.

One word he'd said had evoked a memory for her, too. It came with the smell of wood smoke.

Creasing. She'd been sitting around the campfire during the cattle drive after she'd first come home from San Francisco. Someone had mentioned creasing, but who? The memory wouldn't focus, but it involved the Phantom.

"I'm not sure I know what you mean by *creasing*," Sam said.

"What?"

"Creasing," she repeated, then shrugged.

"It was a long time ago, little girl, so don't get your back up. If a man was a good shot, creasin' was the quickest way to catch one of them crowbaits and not have to spend all day chasin, wearin' it down."

Crowbait was another creepy term you didn't hear everyday, Sam thought. She couldn't imagine killing a wild horse and using his body to attract crows, which some ranchers considered pests.

Sam listened for the faint hum of Mr. Blair's tape recorder to make sure she was getting every word, but Caleb was talking again.

"Yessir, you'd see one you liked and—bing!"

Caleb Sawyer made a sawing motion across the back of his own neck.

"Just nick it, see? Between the mane and withers. Some kinda nerve's there. Don't hurt 'em a bit. Paralyzes 'em, though, and gives ya plenty of time to get 'em hog-tied. If you do it right."

Sam recoiled. How often had it been done wrong?

She imagined a tangle of hooves and hide colliding with the desert floor. How many horses had died of broken necks? How many had lain with terrified eyes, unable to fight back?

"'Course, that was a lifetime ago." Caleb's gaze sharpened, but then he tantalized her with more. "Small planes, now, that's the way to run 'em down. I told Slocum that."

Slocum again. And they'd discussed catching wild horses! Please let that tape be turning, recording every ugly word.

"You mean the helicopters, like the BLM uses?"

Caleb shook his head and spat in the dust.

Sam stepped back, then checked to make sure Jen and Ryan hadn't abandoned her. They hadn't.

"'Course not." His bleary eyes seemed to focus. "Slocum wanted that white stud, the one you saw me scare the other day. All I did was spook him. No one can say different. You were there. You know that."

Sam gave a grudging nod. Sawyer was probably right. If there'd been a drop of blood on the Phantom, she would have seen it.

"He come to me, Slocum did. Offered me enough money to tempt a saint, but I told him I was out of the wild horse huntin' business. Then he asked all these same questions you are, like how it was done in the old days. And I told him."

A flicker of emotion crossed the old man's face. Disgust? Regret? Maybe he had a conscience, Sam thought.

"Heard he tried some of it. Fool city slicker. I got no use for him, 'cept maybe to save myself a trip to the bank, know what I mean?"

He laughed until he started coughing. "I'd like to fill those tents again," he said, nodding at them. "Lead a huntin' party after them buffalo."

Sam had heard Slocum's buffalo were headed for a preserve somewhere, but why should she tell the hermit?

"If you knew he was so incompetent, why did you tell him how to do those things?" Sam demanded. "You must have known he'd only hurt the horses."

"You remind me of another sassy woman. 'Harmin' the horses,' that's what she accused me of when she come out here. Three or four times it was and leave here mad, every time."

Sam's heart thundered so hard it felt like her rib cage vibrated. It had been Mom. Absolutely.

"Still, I didn't mind havin' her come around." Caleb Sawyer fell quiet.

Why hadn't he shut up before uttering those last words? Everything had been black and white.

"It's the honest truth, little girl, those were different days. I ain't taken a horse in years."

She had no reason to believe him, but she did. And this was not the ending she wanted. Old, deaf, kind to his dog, and, in a way, he'd admired Mom.

But she hated what he'd done to the mustangs. She couldn't forgive him his past. What if his horse hunting days weren't over?

"I don't see any cattle." Sam tried once more to trap him. "How do you make a living?"

"Saved some cash from the old days, if it's any business of yours, which it ain't. Now and then I still take hunters out for antelope. That's why I was scarin' off that herd. Why share the feed for my cash crop of pronghorn?"

"You could keep them out by—"

"Man shouldn't have to fence his land," he interrupted, gazing over her shoulder.

"But it's against the law. Even if you don't shoot

the horses, it's called harassment and — "

"I know about those fool laws," he said, fluttering both hands her way, as if she were a pesky hen. "Before you go plannin' my jail time, you ask that red-headed woman about statutes of limitations."

Sam was trying to unravel the hermit's words when a horn blasted behind her.

When she turned around, a white truck was pulling up beside Slocum's. Its red-haired driver flung the door open, slipped out, then slammed it so hard, the BLM truck shuddered.

Sam had never been afraid of Brynna, but now she saw that was a mistake.

Chapter Fifteen ∽

$\mathcal{C}$aleb Sawyer greeted Brynna as if he knew her, then guffawed until he was out of breath as Brynna ordered Sam into her truck.

As if she were a child, Sam thought. As if she didn't have this tape, which could get Caleb Sawyer thrown in jail!

Humiliated and angry, Sam did as she was told. At least Ryan and Jen had left when Brynna arrived. Given Jen's level of curiosity, Sam thought, that proved once again that Jen was an amazing friend.

Brynna shifted into reverse, turned the truck around, then aimed it at each rut as if she welcomed the hammering impact.

"All the way over here I was kicking myself for

not trusting you," Brynna said. "Now I see why I came anyway. You lied to me."

A click sounded from Sam's pocket. Mr. Blair's tape recorder had lasted long enough to record her disgrace.

"I didn't," Sam said, pointing out the camera around her neck as if it were a witness. "And you won't believe all the stuff he told me."

"Oh yes, I will, because I was already here today. And I probably asked him the same questions!" Brynna gave a self-mocking smile. "To think I was going to give you all my notes, just like a present, while we ate our pizza."

If Brynna already knew everything, and she hadn't had Caleb Sawyer arrested, that couldn't be good.

"Don't you think he's guilty?" Sam asked quietly.

"I'm quite certain he is guilty," Brynna snapped. "But it will take a while to prove it."

"I've got him saying a lot of stuff on tape," Sam offered. "If it would help."

"That's not what you should be worrying about," Brynna said. "You've gone too far this time, Sam, and I don't know what we're going to do. Obviously *grounding* doesn't hold any great terror for you."

Sam braced her elbows on her thighs and put her face in her hands. Maybe she could think of some punishment awful enough that they wouldn't send her away.

"You're not even sorry, are you?" Brynna demanded.

"Let me play this tape for you. Then you'll see—"

"That's not the point, Samantha. You're not listening to me."

"Professional journalists do it and it stands up in court," Sam insisted.

"You won't even use the sense an animal does, to keep itself safe," Brynna said. "Didn't you feel creepy walking toward his cabin? I know you did, but you kept going."

Once they were back on a paved road, the windstorm Ryan had mentioned materialized.

Wispy dust devils swept across the range, carrying sand and small pieces of brush.

"Whatever we do will be for your own good," Brynna said.

She sounded hard and final, and Sam didn't know what to do.

Peering from the truck, she saw the sky overhead was still blue, but more clouds had rolled in. Once, a violent patter of raindrops almost obscured vision through the windshield. Next, there was a rumble of thunder, but the storm passed in minutes, leaving only the wind behind.

"We don't know if Caleb Sawyer is dangerous," Brynna burst out. She'd kept brooding, Sam guessed, as they drove along. "It's not the lie as much as a total lack of judgment. Why couldn't you wait?"

Sam shook her head. She'd wanted to save the day, to identify and catch the bad guy Mom had been after. Why couldn't they see that?

"You have to listen to this tape," Sam said again. "He mentions my mom. He said . . ."

Brynna's sigh rocked her whole body. Her mouth was downturned and sad. "You're just not getting it, Sam. We're talking about two different things, and one of them is your safety."

Was it babyish to wish someone would comfort, not punish her? Sam wondered. All she wanted to do was put her arms around Ace's neck and cry.

A house-high whirlwind spun before the truck as Brynna drove across the bridge and into the ranch yard.

At the hitching rail, Dad was unsaddling Strawberry. He raised his forearm to shield his eyes from the blowing sand.

He didn't smile or wave.

It figured. Dad had already had a difficult day and it was about to get worse.

Please don't send me away. I can't stand it. Half of her wanted to run to Dad and beg. The other half wanted to rage that it was unfair. The words tumbled through her mind again and again. *Please, don't make me go.*

Stubbornness kept her from begging, but how long would pride last against the soaring Calico Mountains, the hawks floating lazily over ridges, the horses, Jen and Jake?

Sam swallowed hard. It felt like a bone had wedged in her throat.

Just when she thought the whirlwind had gone, it was back, carrying something blue.

"What in the world . . . ?" Brynna said, but Sam knew instantly.

The tarp. Dad had told her to weight down the tarp with rocks, so it wouldn't blow away. She'd meant to . . . She was going to . . .

And there it went.

"Oh no!" Brynna gasped and slammed on the brakes. She was out of the truck and running by the time Sam realized the tarp, crackling and snapping in the wind, was swooping like a giant blue bat over Penny's corral.

All of the horses heard the tarp. When they saw it, they fled for the far end of the ten-acre pasture. Penny could only hear it, but she tried to follow the others.

"Stop, oh stop," Sam stood next to the truck, arms raised as if she could snag it from the air or will it back to earth.

Penny's neigh of terror cut Sam like a knife. The blind sorrel fled after the sound of the stampeding hooves, but her corral was small and made of pipe.

Metal rang with the impact of the mare's front legs. She stumbled backward and fell.

Instantly, she struggled to her feet. Her head swung between Brynna's voice and the running hooves. Then the tarp rustled again, as it drifted to the ground, and Penny tried to batter her way through the fence.

"Brynna, stop!" Dad's voice was louder than the mare's screams. The fringe on his chaps swirled as he threw himself over the fence and into the pipe corral ahead of Brynna.

Arms spread, speaking calmly, he approached the blind mare. "Whoa, there, whoa."

Sam heard him make a clucking sound and so did Penny. Brynna hung on the fence, panting for breath. The short sprint and total panic had taken everything out of her, but she trusted Dad to help her horse.

Sam stood frozen. One of the pipe panels veed out from the weight of the mare's body, crashing her delicate forelegs into the metal.

The cuts on Penny's front legs began to bleed. Sam longed to cover them with her own hands, but that would only frighten the mare more.

Before Dad reached Penny, another sound set her off. Pushed by the wind, the tarp scuttled along the ground.

Penny galloped around the pen. Her shoulder struck one panel and she ricocheted toward the far side of her pen. At last, she stood, ears back, ribs working in and out. But when Brynna called her name, Penny pricked her ears toward her mistress's voice.

"You're okay, Penny. We'll help you."

What should I do? Sam wondered. Go gather the tarp and fold it so it couldn't do more damage? Or would that sound cause the mare to hurt herself more? And just what was it that had been so important that she couldn't do what Dad had asked?

Penny pawed with a front hoof, then stood, holding it clear of the ground. Dad stood back. Tense and watchful, he braced, ready to dart forward and catch Penny's halter.

Sam edged close to the corral.

"Dad, should I get the tarp?" she whispered.

He shook his head. "Thanks, honey, but leave it for now."

Thanks, *honey*? Had he forgotten . . . ? And then Sam realized he had. Dad didn't remember telling her to deal with the tarp.

Dad's mouth drooped at each corner and his shoulders sagged. Not now. If she confessed now, she'd only drag him down farther.

A crow flew overhead, giving a raucous caw. Penny shied, but stayed near Brynna.

Sam clung to the fence with hands like claws. She watched Dallas come with first aid supplies and bandages. She heard Dad swear it was a bad luck day all around. He'd found Buttercup dead and spent all afternoon searching for her calf.

"Two lost," Dad muttered, referring to the cow and calf. Then he looked at Penny. "At least it wasn't three."

Brynna's eyes swung to Sam. Dad had been talking about Penny, but she knew her stepmother was thinking about Caleb Sawyer. He hadn't been dangerous, but what if he had?

Brynna didn't tell Dad what Sam had done, not yet. She held Penny's halter, petting and crooning to her while Dad cleaned, medicated, and bandaged the sorrel's legs.

The kitchen was quiet when Sam went inside the house. Not until then did she remember Gram had her garden club meeting at the Darton library tonight. Dinner wasn't made. She and Brynna were supposed to bring home pizza for Dad.

Sam sighed. She'd messed that up, too. Why *wouldn't* they send her away? She hurried upstairs. Before anyone could come after her, she ran a deep bath.

She took off her horsehair bracelet and sank in up to her collarbone. She stared at the bathroom ceiling. After a while, she realized she was singing "The Itsy Bitsy Spider."

How dumb was that? She'd lied to her stepmother. She'd hurt a sweet, defenseless horse, and here she was, nearly fourteen and singing a baby song. And then she remembered why.

She couldn't have been more than three or four when she had a high fever and the doctor had advised Mom to keep her in a cool bath. She'd hated it. Even now she remembered how she'd shivered, teeth clacking together, but Mom had sung to her. How many verses did "Itsy Bitsy Spider" have, anyway? Or had Mom been making them up to comfort her?

She tried not to remember what Jake had said the other day. He'd been talking about Brynna trusting him to go check out Caleb Sawyer's complaint.

If people believe in you, you can either disappoint them or measure up.

In trying to please her mom, she'd let everyone around her down. She didn't know how to fix it, because she wasn't all wrong and she couldn't say she was.

A sharp rap sounded on the bathroom door and Dad called through it. "You come on down and eat."

"I'm not hungry," she said, then grimaced at her own lame excuse.

"Come out anyway. Other people need to shower, and you and I need to talk."

His angry voice told Sam that Brynna had told Dad everything.

"Just tell me," Sam shouted back. She hoped he didn't hear the sound of her hands coming out of the water to cover her eyes for the second time today.

"If that's the way you want it," he said. "You're staying home tomorrow. We're riding out at dawn and expect you to have dinner on the table when we get home. Then we'll talk about what happens next. I'm giving myself twenty-four hours to think, because right now —"

Dad broke off. Sam kept listening.

"Samantha!" Dad snapped. "Did you hear me?"

"Yes sir," she said. "I'll do what you said."

After Dad's boots clomped back down the stairs, Sam climbed out of the tub, dried off, and went to her room.

Even though her room was warm from sunlight streaming through the window all day, she pulled on sweatpants and a sweatshirt. Not her emerald green Darton High sweats, but the faded, washed-a-million-times, red ones from her old San Francisco middle school.

When she could hear the television downstairs, Sam replayed the tape very quietly. What could she find to put Caleb in jail, to prove she'd done the right thing by going there?

The part about being a bison guide wasn't illegal. The part where he discussed creasing and water trapping wild horses was illegal now, but had it been when he'd done it?

Wait. Was Caleb Sawyer old enough to have done it when it was legal? And what if he'd lied?

In despair, Sam played the tape over again. Someone who knew a lot more about law needed to listen. Even that part where Sawyer admitted giving Linc Slocum advice about catching wild horses wasn't a sure thing.

He could be an accessory to Slocum's crime. Still, even though everyone around knew Slocum was responsible for that scar on the Phantom's neck, no one had been able to prove it.

Sam sighed. She had to find a way to get Brynna and Dad to listen to the tape.

She was still awake when she heard Gram's yellow Buick come over the River Bend Bridge and park in the yard. She heard Gram talking with Brynna, but only caught a couple of words about how early they'd get up in the morning.

The house grew silent and Sam kept staring at the ceiling. She didn't imagine prancing horses on it tonight. She felt heartsick and hopeless.

"I can't go back," she whispered into the darkness.

It was all she thought about until midnight, when she heard a stallion call from the wild side of the river.

Chapter Sixteen ❧

Had she really heard him? Or had she wished so hard for the stallion to come that she'd imagined his neigh?

Sam sat up. For hours, she'd been lying on top of her covers, staring at the ceiling, seeing nothing. Now, she closed her eyes, focusing on the silence.

Cougar mewed from outside her closed bedroom door. When she didn't answer his summons, he batted at the door, trying to slip his paw beneath it. Could she have been dozing and heard that?

No. She hadn't been asleep. She noticed the glow from her wristwatch. Twelve twenty-seven. Whenever the Phantom came to the river, it was about this time. And yet no neigh followed the first.

Sam drew a breath. She was going down there.

She glanced around her room for her horsehair bracelet. She'd left it in the bathroom and it would cause too much commotion to go after it.

She was looking at the little tape when she heard Cougar complain again. What if he thought the tape was a toy? She could imagine him batting it across the floor, so she slipped it into her pocket and stepped toward her bedroom door.

A floorboard squeaked. So did her door hinge. She was three steps down the staircase when she heard the rustle of sheets. Then came Dad's voice, not a bit sleepy.

"Let her go. She can sleep tomorrow when we're gone."

Sam swallowed her sigh. She knew why Dad hadn't stopped her. Last summer, he'd told her that when she was a fussy baby, Mom had taken her to listen to the rush and gurgle of the La Charla River. The river's age-old conversation with the river rocks had always lulled her to sleep.

Since Dad had told her, she'd often gone down to the river and its magic always worked.

She had to believe that was why. Otherwise, it was possible Dad was letting her say good-bye.

With something like permission on her side, Sam didn't worry about the sound of every footfall. Once in the kitchen, she snagged a muffin from Gram's bread box and two packets of string cheese from the refrigerator. She'd missed dinner, hiding out in her room, and she was starving.

If it turned out that the Phantom really wasn't at the river, she'd sit there and have a lonely picnic just the same.

She started to stuff the food in the pocket of her sheepskin-lined leather coat and realized her sweat-pants' pocket held the tape recorder.

Her heart double-thumped at the idea that she might go into the river to touch the Phantom. That would definitely be bad for Mr. Blair's tape recorder, though, so she left it on the kitchen table.

With those moments lost, she crammed the food into her coat pockets, hurried to tug on the barn boots she kept by the door, then slipped into the warm almost-summer night.

Diamond-bright stars and a half-moon mottled pewter and white seemed to dangle from the black sky like ornaments. With quick, quiet steps, she crossed the bridge. Blaze must be sound asleep in the bunkhouse, she thought.

She was almost across when she saw the mustangs. They poured down the mountainside like water. Before reaching the river they stopped, bumping shoulders and making low whinnies as their leader stepped into the clear.

I couldn't have heard him, Sam thought. *He wasn't here.*

Sam shivered. It wasn't the first time the bond she shared with the stallion had amazed her.

If only she could live with the mustangs, all her problems wouldn't matter.

The Phantom emerged from the herd of darker horses. He stood alone, facing her across the river, but he wasn't watching her. He focused on safety.

Herd stallions tested the water while their band stayed back, ready to run if he encountered trouble. The Phantom was no different.

Standing tall, he stared upstream. His ears were pricked to listen and his nostrils flared. His front hooves danced in place as he looked downstream. Sensing no predators, he lowered his nose to the water, took a sip, then swerved and returned to his band.

With a cranky squeal, he drove them forward, snapping at the tails of stragglers.

Sam smiled. The Phantom was in a hurry tonight, and his band knew it. They drank long and loud, until a big honey-colored mare backed from the water. The others copied her movements, then milled in confusion. For all his haste, the stallion hadn't given the order to depart.

Suddenly, Sam realized what the herd's appearance meant. At least for tonight, they'd left Antelope Crossing and returned to their usual territory. On the lands bordering River Bend Ranch, the horses were safe.

The Phantom shouldered through his herd, heading back to the river. He waded in as deep as his knees, then stopped.

Although he wouldn't be milk white for years, he'd shed his thick winter coat, and his skin looked silken and pearly in the moonlight.

River rocks gleamed black as he picked around each one, making his way into deeper water, where the strong current had pushed the rocks tumbling downstream. Once he reached the smoother footing, he trotted toward Sam. Water droplets flew up around his knees, catching moonlight and sparkling before they fell.

"Zanzibar," Sam whispered.

Snow-melt cold, the river surrounded her boots, flowing past, rising with each step until her sweatpants were wet and soggy to the knees. Sam didn't care. Each stride she took matched one of the stallion's. They'd meet in the middle.

But then he stopped. His reflection shone on the glossy wavelets and the stallion trembled with wariness. Had he heard something, or was the Phantom reminding himself he was wild? He gathered himself and Sam felt sure he'd flee. Instead, he launched forward, creating a white-capped wave, and then he stood within her reach.

A nicker shook him. His tangled forelock didn't hide the stallion's brown eyes.

He must remember the days she'd spent schooling him in the river.

Here, she'd mounted him for the first time. Though it had been a hot summer day almost three years ago, tension and excitement still vibrated in this place.

But there was danger in thinking this animal was just an old friend, and Sam knew it.

Powerful muscles showed like the fretting in a thundercloud as the stallion pawed the river, splashing her.

"Careful," Sam said. Was she talking to the horse or herself? He was a wild stallion. She could never let herself forget that.

But he'd come to her tonight, when she was heartsick, when she wanted more than anything to feel part of the rangeland she might have to leave.

Twice, the great stallion had let her ride him.

Tonight, she'd ask him again.

Sam held her hand palm up. Inches above her hand, Zanzibar breathed in her scent, then snorted and backed away.

His hooves grated on river rocks as he moved off. He was about halfway back to his herd when he stopped and studied her.

He was thinking, making a decision. Sam held her breath. She'd looked into the eyes of almost every horse she'd met. Most horses acted on instinct, but sometimes, she was sure, the Phantom thought.

He moved so quickly, then, muscles bunching and shifting beneath his silver hide, that Sam splashed, getting out of his way.

But the stallion had evaluated her and decided she was no threat. He moved through the water in front of her and stopped, facing upstream.

Jake had held a black colt in just that position when she'd mounted him for the first time.

"That's an invitation, boy," she warned him. "Are you sure?"

The stallion looked back over his shoulder, then swished his tail impatiently.

Sam looked back at the ranch. Not a light shone. All lay in sleepy darkness. They had no idea what she was about to do. Even she didn't know where the stallion would take her. But how could she say no?

Sam leaned her weight against him. If he changed his mind, it would happen now. She smoothed her hands over his back and barrel. His skin shivered, but he stood firm.

Sam held her breath. With a hop and a bound, grabbing a handful of mane, she vaulted onto the stallion's back.

He reared.

"Oh no, boy." Sam shifted her weight forward, burying both hands in his mane, laying her cheek along his neck until he came back down.

His hind legs lashed out. His back rose and he bucked. The sky was a starry blue-black smear. Sam's teeth clacked together.

Was he playing, or fighting her unfamiliar weight?

All at once, the stallion whirled toward shore. The far shore. Legs tight against his body, arms clamped along his neck, Sam stayed astride.

A hoof slipped on river rock, but he didn't fall.

Splashing, crashing through the water, he gained the shore and then they were in the midst of the mares.

Startled snorts greeted them.

Both times Sam had been on his back, they'd been alone, but suddenly she was part of the herd. No more, no less.

Hot hide brushed her legs. Muscles and heat surrounded her as she lay along the stallion's neck, feeling the rough texture of his mane in her hands.

Whatever sign he gave, she missed it. The herd didn't; they settled into a smooth run, flowing around rocks and stunted piñon pines. Sam imagined she was a centaur. Half girl, half merged into this river of horses.

She didn't miss reins or stirrups or even the sight of what was up ahead, beyond the horses.

The star-smeared sky slipped by. Wind-tangled mane lashed around her with the sharp scent of crushed sagebrush. The Phantom knew where to go. Sam never wanted to stop.

She couldn't say how long they galloped, but when the huffing herd slowed, they didn't stop. They trotted steadily uphill.

Only once did her balance falter. Riding by instinct, she hadn't anticipated the narrow ravine. When the stallion jumped, she wasn't ready. She slipped to his right side, about to fall, and the stallion slowed.

With a graceful sidestep, he caught her. Sam smiled as the stallion adjusted his gait and arranged his smooth back beneath her.

Hooves echoed on rock and Sam knew where she was. She hugged closer still to the Phantom's neck. Her cheek felt the sleek new summer coat. The tunnel closed around her.

Ahead, the mares were streaked with moonlight sifting through the fissures in the stone above. Cold rock scuffed her right leg. When she instinctively drew away, her legs tightened against the silver stallion. He bolted against the horses in front of him.

Squeals echoed around her, but she clung to the stallion. If she sat up, her head would strike the hard rock ceiling.

Soon they'd be in the Phantom's secret valley. No one could find her there. She didn't know whether to be frightened or elated.

Hooves thudded and moved away. They were there.

Just as she remembered, rock walls soared up to a dizzying dome of stars. The stallion stopped and started to shake.

Oh no. Sam slipped from his back and stumbled, catching herself against a boulder, before he sprinted away.

Dark horse shadows moved in a meadow where the grass smelled green and sweet even to her human senses. Without her eyes to call the horses bay and black, paint and roan, her ears took over.

Every animal had a different sound. A nicker rose high and inquisitive, but most horses talked in low snorts. Hooves shuffled as favorite spots were claimed. She heard a jumble of limbs hitting the soil as a foal settled down to sleep.

This is heaven, Sam thought.

Just then, two mustangs disagreed. Hooves thudded on hide and teeth snapped. Too close, she thought, crowding back against the valley wall. Then her view was blocked.

Soundless as a cloud, the stallion stood between Sam and the bickering mustangs. Intimidated by his presence, they moved off.

Sam felt along the rocks and found a safe spot. It was not really a cave, but a sort of grotto in the valley wall. She sat, drew her legs up, and curled into it.

She wanted to see the horses. At the first sign of daylight, she'd fill her eyes with this scene most people never witnessed, but she was suddenly exhausted.

It was hard to believe that it had been only this morning that Jen had hugged her and begged her not to be angry. Then there had been Rachel's outburst and Caleb Sawyer, eyes filled with memories of her mother. Brynna looking betrayed. And Dad, sounding so disappointed she'd hidden from him.

If the tape of Caleb Sawyer didn't convince them she'd been smart, not foolhardy, she'd probably be banished to San Francisco. She was already in bigger trouble than she'd ever been in before and if they found out she'd spent the night with the Phantom's herd, she was dead.

Nearby, a coyote's melancholy wail echoed her feelings.

Sam put her hands palm to palm, making a pillow for herself as she leaned against the sun-warmed rock. She'd work it all out in the morning.

Chapter Seventeen ⟋

$\mathcal{D}$aybreak showed Sam a valley full of foals.

"Three, four," Sam counted aloud. From her niche in the cliff wall, she couldn't see them all, so she stood. She spotted two bays, a sorrel, a leggy seal-brown colt that looked older than the others, and a creamy foal that might darken into buckskin. "Five!"

Unafraid but wary, the horses flowed away from her excited voice and movements.

The Phantom trotted toward her, snorting. This morning, he looked every inch a wild stallion. It was hard to believe she'd ridden him.

"Hey, boy," she called.

The stallion didn't greet her. In fact, she might have

been a crack in the canyon wall for all the attention she got.

Hands on hips, Sam watched him go.

This was the horse she'd wanted to protect, Sam thought, shaking her head. Once in a while he needed her help, but this time, he'd done just fine without her.

The Phantom's herd had returned to the valley where he was king.

What would happen if *she* stayed? The idea flared in Sam's mind like a Fourth of July sparkler. Last night, she'd been part of the herd. Even now, the mares and foals weren't afraid. Once they got used to her, they might accept her as one of them.

She'd disappointed her other family, but here she could have a fresh start. And Dad and Brynna couldn't send her back to San Francisco if they couldn't find her.

Sam stared after the Phantom. The early morning sun flowed over a coat wet from rolling in the dew. Along his flanks faint dapples shone like silver coins.

Just ahead of him, two yearlings cried out in defiance. One was a sturdy black youngster. The other was Pirate, the colt with the patch of white over one eye. Locked in mock battle, they fenced with their front legs and didn't notice their sire until Pirate backed into him.

The stallion nipped both colts and gave them such a glare, they retreated across the valley. Heads lowered, they sneaked glances at the Phantom, asking forgiveness, but as long as he stared at them, they stayed away.

If she stayed, would she have to learn mustang rules? Could she?

Sam glanced around this mustang kingdom. She hadn't done so well in her own world, where she knew the language. Even now, she might be in more trouble than she had been when the Phantom had come to meet her at the river.

At home, Dad and the others would have ridden out by now. If they hadn't noticed she was gone, they wouldn't know for hours. She might be able to make it back before they noticed.

How far had the herd galloped last night? Five miles? Ten?

Pirate took a hesitant step toward his father. The Phantom's ears flicked back and his eyes narrowed. Even though he was yards away, Pirate once more lowered his head in disgrace.

Sam drew a breath. No matter how far she'd ridden the Phantom last night, his kingly attitude told her she was returning home afoot. The stallion was in no mood for nonsense.

Sam worked the flattened muffin from her coat pocket. It smelled a little like leather and was vaguely football shaped, but she nibbled as she approached the stream that meandered through the valley.

Cool grass brushed her sweatpants and the sound of horses' teeth ripping and grinding was all around her. At streamside she knelt, splashed water on her face, then cupped her hands to take a drink.

She was swallowing when she saw the tadpoles. Hundreds of the wiggly black things danced in the shadow of the stream bank. Her throat tightened, thinking what might have happened if she'd swallowed one, but then, as she studied the infant frogs, Sam caught her own image in the water.

The clouds overhead shifted. The stream's surface reflected her face as clearly as a mirror and she gasped in surprise.

Arms braced on the bank, Sam lowered her face until it almost touched the water. Her auburn hair fell over each shoulder, giving the impression of pigtails. If she wove in a few daisies, she'd look just like Mom.

Why did that make her feel so weird?

She wanted to be like Mom, didn't she?

Sam swallowed hard. Because no one could listen to her thoughts, she admitted it: not exactly.

Mom had taught her to draw stars and hearts and write her name. Mom had shown her she was loved, and taught her how to love back.

But Mom should have cared as much for herself as she did for wild animals. She'd followed her heart without listening to her head. She should have done both, balancing between the two.

Sam sighed. She often did the same thing—neglecting that tarp, for instance, because she was obsessed with finding Caleb. Going out to Caleb's house when it could have been dangerous.

And now, running away. She hadn't meant to do it, but she'd known when she vaulted onto the Phantom's back that he'd take her far from home.

Sam sat back on her heels. At least Mom had had an excuse for her wayward heart. She'd been raised in the city and couldn't get enough of wild Nevada. Too late, she'd learned that the wilderness didn't forgive mistakes.

But she wasn't all Mom.

Sam felt her lips lift in a smile as she imagined her heritage, described in equine terms. *By dependable, common-sense Wyatt, out of wild, softhearted Louise.* She had the bloodlines to be a real cowgirl; she just had to learn how.

She focused on the tadpoles again.

"I'm really glad I didn't slurp up one of you guys," she said. As she watched their watery, wiggly dance, a shadow fell over her.

Big and silent, the Phantom lowered his head to drink and her reflection wavered, mixing with his silver one.

"Hey, boy."

The stallion drew his dripping lips from the water. He stamped and fixed her with accusing eyes.

"What?" she asked him. "You brought me here."

His mane scattered in a hundred directions as he shook his head, then backed away.

Sam chuckled. It was time for her to go home.

* * *

The Phantom didn't watch her leave, but Sam didn't mind. When you're friends with a mustang, she told herself, you've got to be forgiving and flexible.

It was just as well, really.

She didn't want to go back to San Francisco. Besides missing all the horses and the ranch, there was her reputation at school. Rachel's tantrum had taken the focus off of Sam, but if she was sent away for the summer, people might jump to the wrong conclusion.

A good night's sleep had made her see it was possible that Brynna, Dad, and Gram would see things her way. Almost. She had the tape to prove she hadn't just blundered onto the hermit's property without a plan. And Brynna needed her help with the HARP program.

Besides, maybe no one knew she'd messed up again. She really might slip home before anyone missed her.

If she'd been riding a wild white stallion, that would have been impossible, but the Phantom had forced her to go alone.

An hour later, Sam had made it through the dark, spooky tunnel, over the shale-strewn hillside, and found her way onto a rough path choked with bitterbrush.

It was only May, and judging by the sun on the eastern horizon, only about eight o'clock. How could it be so hot? She shrugged out of her coat and tied it around her waist.

By the time she figured she was halfway home, her feet hurt. She wasn't limping yet, but it wouldn't be long. Barn boots weren't designed for long hikes.

Sam forgot all about her aching feet when she heard the coyotes yipping.

She'd noticed them last night, but these sounds were different. High-pitched and excited, these were the calls of hunters. They were after something.

Sam burst into a jog. A shower of sand shot from under her boots. She slipped and sat down hard on the desert floor.

Think, she told herself, *then act.*

Coyotes were rarely dangerous to humans, but did she really have any idea what she was running toward? She took a deep breath and held it while she thought.

As a matter of fact, she did know what she was about to run into.

Trouble.

Fighting her desire to rush, Sam scanned the terrain ahead.

There. A copse of cottonwood trees lay about a quarter mile away. Two coyotes, coats shining in shades of black and tan, bobbed around a boulder. One darted in, then the other. They had something.

"Hey! Get out of there!" Sam shouted.

The coyotes spun to face her. Both tails wagged low as if they were embarrassed. When Sam took one step closer, the coyotes bounded away.

They couldn't have been too hungry, Sam thought.

And then she heard a calf bawl.

As she made her way toward it, Sam wondered what kind of mother cow left her baby alone. And neglected to teach it to be quiet. Coyotes weren't the only predators that relished calves for breakfast, and humans were almost never around as guardians.

For that reason, Sam stayed watchful. If the cow was nearby, she could charge. Pointed hooves backed by a ton of angry mother wasn't a challenge she wanted to face.

Almost there, she still hadn't seen another living thing. In fact, there was no boulder or bush big enough to hide a cow.

The calf was alone, curled beside a rock, under a cottonwood tree.

The calf looked up. Wide trusting eyes stared out of a curly white face. It licked its pink nose as if searching for one last drop of milk. She was the tiniest calf Sam had ever seen: half the size Buddy had been as a baby.

Suddenly Sam noticed the calf's unusual yellow coloring and her heart fell.

This was Buttercup's calf—and Buttercup was dead.

"Poor little thing," Sam said out loud.

The calf bawled again as if urging her to do something.

Dad had buried Buttercup yesterday. That meant the calf had been without nourishment for a full day, and that was far too long.

Gram kept a powdered formula for infant calves in the pantry. Dad had more of it on a shelf in the tack room. There were simple directions for mixing it with water, but first she had to get Buttercup's baby home.

"Ready for a ride, cutie?" Sam asked the calf.

She decided to take its bleat for "yes."

Gingerly, Sam worked her arms under the tiny calf. Weak as she was, the calf still struggled. Sam held her firmly, letting her delicate legs dangle free.

"Comfy?" Sam asked, realizing the little calf was much heavier than she looked.

With one last wiggle, she looked into Sam's face, blinked her white eyelashes, and fell asleep.

As she trudged along carrying the calf, Sam realized that all week, she'd been trying to give her mother something for Mother's Day.

Revenge was what she'd been hoping for, but now, she held the perfect gift. This little calf—not vengeance—was exactly what Mom would have wanted.

Sam paused to shift the calf into a more secure position. She let herself take a couple of normal breaths and waited for her pulse to quit pounding in her wrists and neck.

Come to think of it, Gram and Brynna would appreciate a little yellow calf a lot more than perfume or scarves, too.

Sam kept walking.

Chapter Eighteen ❧

Sam's feet in their sloppy-fitting barn boots told her she'd walked about a hundred miles, but her brain said it was probably only five or six.

Just as bad was the fact that the no-see-'ems were back. She didn't know the scientific name for the little biting insects, but Gram fussed at them all through the spring and summer, saying they pestered her when she was gardening.

Once, when they were very young, Jake had told Sam that the itchy little bugs drank sweat. Yuck. She could almost believe it.

Now she felt them crawling through the roots of her hair. They must be working up an appetite playing safari, Sam thought, because they stopped every couple of minutes to take a bite of her scalp.

Why hadn't she worn her Stetson?

Oh yeah, because she'd only been walking down to the river. . . .

Sam sighed. That wild ride on the Phantom was worth any price, but she still wished she'd see a driver or rider, someone to help her carry this orphan calf back to the ranch.

She couldn't even hear La Charla yet. She was hot, cranky, and ready to be home. So was Daisy.

She wasn't sure when she'd started calling the yellow calf Daisy, but she knew why. It was partly because she came from a long line of flower-named cows, starting with Petunia; partly for the daisies mom had worn in her braids; and partly because cows with names were less likely to become hamburgers.

Not that Daisy appreciated the favor.

A couple of miles back, Sam had stopped to catch her breath and the little calf had drawn back a dangling hind hoof and kicked her in the stomach. Since then, every time Sam stopped, Daisy kicked her again.

Hoping to soothe Daisy into napping again, Sam began singing. She sang "Twinkle, Twinkle Little Star."

Daisy seemed to like it, so Sam kept adding verses.

> *"I have had it little cow.*
> *Every step makes me say 'ow.'*
> *Icky bugs are eating me,*

> *Like I was a ripe green pea.*
> *I have had it little cow.*
> *Every step makes me say 'ow.'"*

Sam sang it again, this time like opera. Daisy didn't care if she listened to it as a tango or country-western, as long as she didn't hear silence.

Daisy's ears fluttered and Sam decided the calf was partial to the verse with a forced rhyme between *Rachel* and *space shuttle*. She was concocting a story about the rich girl orbiting an undiscovered planet, when a different verse popped into her head.

> *"Stupid Jake, you low-down snake,*
> *Always eating my gram's cake.*
> *You could drive by any time,*
> *But you act like that's a crime.*
> *Stupid Jake you low-down snake,*
> *Always eating my gram's cake."*

Really, where *was* Jake when you needed him? He didn't even have to be driving. She'd seen him carry a foal across his saddle. He could carry a calf. And she'd ridden double with him two weeks ago when he was tracking Star, so why couldn't he return the favor?

Sam looked left and right. Nothing. Jake had five brothers, for crying out loud! Didn't they ever go anywhere?

Or Ryan. Ryan was a good sport. Even if he was driving Linc's Cadillac, he'd let her and Daisy ride in air-conditioned comfort all the way home.

At this point she'd even settle for Mrs. Allen's tangerine-colored truck, though Mrs. Allen was the worst driver in northern Nevada, maybe in the whole state, and possibly in the entire country.

I'll take my chances, Sam thought, but just then she saw the highway and heard the La Charla River.

She stopped, took a deep breath, and then—oof!

"I'm walking, Daisy," she told the calf, once she could talk again. "And I've come up with a plan to make a bad guy just as uncomfortable as I am.

"Ow, okay," she groaned as the calf struck again. "We're almost home, baby, almost home."

Buddy stood at the fence of the ten-acre pasture, sniffing. Her nostrils flared and her eyes rolled as if Daisy's scent was the most wonderful smell in the world.

Maybe Buddy really did miss living with cows.

Quietly, Sam clucked her tongue at Buddy and she gave a lonely moo.

"Shh," Sam told Buddy. "You can play with her later. Just don't wake her up, now."

Buddy ran along the fence, bucking in delight.

Sam felt a little guilty. If only the range didn't have predators and mean old cows to kick a newcomer just to teach her who was boss.

As Sam turned toward the house, Buddy bawled pitifully.

Daisy's eyes opened wide. She began kicking, twisting, and struggling to put her feet on the ground.

Sam shouldered open the screen door. It almost slammed closed, striking her elbow. Using her fingers from beneath Daisy's body, she got the front door open, though, and kicked it closed behind her.

She was barely inside the cool, welcoming kitchen when she noticed the tape of her talk with Caleb Sawyer had been taken out of the tape player. A note sat beside it.

Sam shifted Daisy to one side and peered past her head, to read.

"Sam—Monday A.M. I'll get a copy of this to Sheriff Ballard. Just in case. B."

They must have listened to it and thought it really was worth something. She didn't dare dance while holding Daisy, but she wanted to.

But what if the sheriff just held onto the tape? Caleb knew she had it, so he probably wouldn't do anything stupid. But Linc Slocum didn't know. What if he did something else to endanger the horses?

"Ow, Daisy!" Sam yelped, then lowered her to the kitchen rug.

She'd have to think about Slocum later.

She darted into the living room, grabbed the afghan off the couch, and slipped back into the kitchen before Daisy had a chance to follow.

Some people, Sam thought as she spread the knit blanket on the kitchen floor, would get mad if their granddaughter brought a calf into the kitchen. But not Gram.

There'd been orphan animals in the house before. As long as she kept things neat, her family would welcome the rescued calf. For a little while.

Daisy dozed while Sam found the bottle, nipple, and calf formula in the pantry, but she woke the yellow calf to feed her. Daisy needed nourishment. After ten minutes of slobbering and splattering them both with formula, she realized it was food and settled down to suckle, then nap some more.

Even though it wasn't close to dinnertime, Sam set out the ingredients for lasagna. Better to start early, she thought. It might take her a while.

Actually, it wasn't that hard to make, she discovered as she chopped and minced and mixed. Maybe she'd inherited Mom's knack for lasagna.

As she cooked, Sam figured out how she'd scare Linc Slocum into behaving. Then, while the meat, garlic, onions, and spices cooked, she put her plan into motion.

"I'm feeling just cranky enough to make this work," Sam whispered to Daisy.

Sam flipped the tape and slipped it back into the tape recorder. She needed an attachment to do this right, but if she held the receiver a little away from her ear, she might be able to catch Linc Slocum's guilty voice.

She opened the phone book and dialed his number. *Don't let Rachel answer,* she thought.

"Slocum," snapped Linc as he picked up the telephone.

Relieved, Sam moved closer to the tape recorder.

"Hi, Mr. Slocum," she began. "This is Samantha Forster."

"Well, Samantha, I ain't heard your voice in a month of Mondays."

Linc Slocum loved silly Western sayings. He thought it made him sound like a cowboy.

It didn't, and Sam was pretty sure the saying was "a month of Sundays." Still, she didn't correct him.

"Mr. Slocum, I'm going to say something I'm afraid you won't like."

"Oh now, what could a sweet little . . ."

As Linc's voice trailed off, Sam guessed he was remembering how she'd sabotaged his attempt to adopt the Phantom the previous summer. Maybe he was thinking of the reward money he'd had to pay her for catching the stallion who'd stolen Hotspot. And, though she'd never proven he'd helped Karla Starr capture the Phantom for a rodeo bucking horse, she'd come close. He might be recalling that.

Or maybe Linc Slocum had learned thirteen-year-old girls weren't as helpless as they looked.

"Here's the thing, Mr. Slocum," she said quietly, watching Daisy to be sure she didn't waken.

"Speak up, girl."

"I'm afraid I can't, Mr. Slocum. There's someone

here who'll be really upset if I do."

In the moment of silence that followed, Sam realized Slocum thought he was being threatened.

"Who is it you're talking about?" he asked. "Your dad? That Jake Ely?"

Sam didn't tell. She just smiled at the harmless yellow calf.

"It doesn't matter, Mr. Slocum," she told him. "The thing is, I was talking with the man who taught you about mustanging. A lot of people suspect you're the one who scarred the Phantom, but he knows it. He taught you how."

For some reason, she thought it would be smarter not to mention Caleb Sawyer's name.

"Hmph," Slocum grumped. "That's one man's word against another's."

"Except I have it on tape," Sam pointed out.

He was quiet again.

"Still," Slocum said at last, less vehemently, "you've got no witnesses."

"Okay. You're right," Sam agreed. "I just thought I'd let you know before I turn this tape over to Sheriff Ballard."

"What?" Slocum's voice was so loud, Sam was afraid he'd wake up Daisy. "What do you think the sheriff'd want with it?"

"I'm not sure," Sam said, trying to sound puzzled. "But I think it's called 'building a body of evidence.' You know, so that if anything happens to the Phantom . . ."

"That's blackmail! And, and," Slocum grasped for words. "Maybe I'm not the one you should be worrying about, little lady!"

"He knew he was speaking on tape," Sam said, still not mentioning Caleb Sawyer by name.

"And he said—" Slocum broke off.

Sam was pretty sure Slocum was weighing his words, now, wondering what Caleb had said about the past and predicted for the future.

That satisfied Sam. She might not have dragged a confession out of Linc Slocum, but self-preservation was supposed to be a deterrent to crime. Now that he knew she had incriminating information about him, he might leave the horses alone.

Her spirits rose. Even though this wasn't a triumph she'd share with her family, the small victory was worth winning.

"Samantha Forster," Linc shouted, "I'll tell you what, if you were a well-behaved young lady like my Rachel, your life would run a lot smoother!"

Sam didn't let herself laugh. She couldn't think of anything she wanted to say on tape, either.

"Good-bye, Mr. Slocum," she said. "It was sure nice talking to you."

It was nearly seven o'clock when Gram, Brynna, and Dad rode into the River Bend Ranch yard.

The lasagna had been done for an hour and it was a little crunchy around the edges.

As Sam opened the door and stood waiting on the

porch, Gram dismounted. Still holding Sweetheart's reins, Gram inhaled deeply.

"Something smells good." She took off her hat and the bandanna she'd worn underneath to protect her gray hair from dust.

Sam's eyes did a quick assessment of her family.

Brynna was loosening Penny's cinch, and running her hands over the mare. Her front legs looked fine.

Dad stood in his stirrups, eyes scanning the rest of the ranch, to see that nothing had gone wrong in his absence.

If they knew she'd been gone all night, they were too tired to say much about it. Yet.

"It does smell good," Brynna agreed, giving Penny a final pat. "You go on in, Grace," she told Gram, "and I'll take care of your horse."

"Before you do," Sam said, standing in the door-way, "you should know we, uh, have a little visitor."

Chapter Nineteen ⤳

Sam's family stood statue still.

Then Gram's head tilted to one side as if she hadn't heard right. Brynna glanced over her shoulder for strange vehicles before she looked at Dad. He dismounted and ground-tied Strawberry.

"Well, shoot," he said, wearily. "I know *I* can't resist goin' in to see."

Quickly, Brynna tied the other horses. As all three of them stepped inside, the calf awoke and blinked her long-lashed eyes.

At the sight of strangers, Daisy bolted to her feet and pressed against Sam's knees. She made a sound that sounded like *maw.*

"This is Daisy," Sam said.

"Buttercup's calf," Dad realized, nodding.

After a quick glance, Brynna wasn't looking at the calf. She was looking at Sam's hair. "Did you spend the night outside?"

Sam touched her hair. It could be full of stickers and burrs for all she knew.

She nodded. Asked a direct question, she just couldn't lie.

"We heard you go out," Dad said. "I woulda been worried if you hadn't been here when we rode in."

"Instead, she's brought us a surprise," Gram said.

Was that all? Sam tried to stay calm, despite her amazement. When all three of them looked happy, she felt guilty instead of relieved.

"I'm really sorry I let you down," she began.

"Honey, you never did," Dad said. "We were only scared for you."

Gram wrapped her in a tight hug. When she finally let go, Sam knew what had to be done next.

"I know how you feel," Sam admitted. "Before I sit down for dinner, I have to take Buddy back out to the herd."

She sighed so loudly, she almost expected them to laugh, but they didn't.

"I'm afraid for her safety," Sam added, "but I know it's what she really wants."

"I think that's a good decision, dear," Gram said.

When Brynna nodded and looked as if she'd put her hat back on, Dad asked, "This somethin' you want to do on your own?"

"Yeah, if it's okay with everybody," Sam said.

"More than okay," Brynna said. "I can't wait to cut a slab of that lasagna."

"Neither can I," Gram said.

"And I'll see how Buttercup's done for us this year," Dad nodded toward Daisy.

Outside, Sam stalled. She put away all three horses, so that Gram, Dad, and Brynna could go ahead and eat.

The sky behind the barn was streaked magenta and purple. There was nothing shy about the end of this day that had started in the Phantom's hidden valley.

Sam made half a dozen trips between the barn and the ranch yard, returning saddles and bridles and collecting grooming tools.

She took her time brushing Ace and saddling him.

At last there was nothing left to do except go to the tack room. For the last time, she took down the little rope halter Dad had fashioned for Buddy.

Alert as a deer, Buddy stood by the pasture fence, waiting. Jeepers-Creepers was rolling in the grass and the other horses were grazing at the far end of the enclosure, but Buddy knew something was up.

Sam glanced at the sky again. She probably had another hour of daylight, so she couldn't use darkness as an excuse to wait one more day.

"And you're not even going to make me play chase, are you?" Sam said, rubbing Buddy's head between the ears, where she liked it best.

Buddy's smooth red ears batted forward and she

ducked her head toward the halter.

"Okay," Sam said quietly. She haltered Buddy, attached a lead rope, led her from the pasture, and swung into Ace's saddle.

In spite of Buddy's excitement, Sam rode past the first knot of cattle gathered about a half mile from the River Bend Bridge.

She let Buddy stop and touch noses, but she kept riding, and though she looked back over her shoulder a few times, Buddy didn't seem too sad to go.

It wouldn't be fair to turn Buddy loose so close to home, anyway.

"I'll tell you why," she said, glancing back at Buddy. "If I'd been able to run home on that first day I met Rachel, I never would have gone back to school. You'll probably feel the same way about some of the cows you meet."

Sam took a breath and though she couldn't believe what she was about to say, she said it anyway. "It's for your own good."

Buddy nodded with each step, so maybe she wasn't agreeing, but Sam decided she was.

Upriver, almost at Three Ponies Ranch, they found a scattering of Herefords with a good mix of young and mature cows. Buddy bucked at the end of the lead rope.

About twenty white faces turned to watch their approach, but only half bolted at the sight of the swinging rope attached to Buddy's halter.

Good, Sam thought. They weren't too wild, but they were skittish enough to run from a potential threat. Buddy would probably be safe with them.

Probably, Sam thought, as she dismounted and ground-tied Ace.

Buddy had stopped pulling at the rope. She still looked curious, but now that Sam was about to set her free, Buddy shifted from hoof to hoof, looking worried.

Ace gave a small nicker. Then the little bay gelding slung his head over Sam's shoulder. He blew through his lips, comforting her.

"Thanks, boy," Sam said.

She walked down the rope, gathering it as she went. She eased the halter over Buddy's ears.

When Buddy didn't buck and run away, Sam couldn't help it: she circled Buddy's neck in a hug, and thought of the day she'd first seen her, alone and trapped in a mire of quicksand.

Buddy's bawling had been low and rough, because her throat was sore from calling for a mother who couldn't come to her.

With Dad's rope tied around her waist, Sam had lain spread-eagled on her belly atop the hot, alkali flat. She'd inched close enough to grab the struggling calf in a bear hug.

Maaaaa, maaaa, Buddy had bawled, but Dad urged his horse away, pulling Buddy from the quicksand as Sam held on tight.

Now, with her face pressed against Buddy's sleek red neck, she held on just as tight.

Sam, you can let go now.

The voice she heard could have been Mom's. It could have been her own, when she was more grown up.

Slowly, Sam loosened her hug. Finally, she let her arms drop away from Buddy's neck.

Buddy hopped a few steps forward. She glanced at Sam, blinking.

Sam took a step back toward Ace and it was all the permission Buddy needed. With a swivel of her heels, Buddy ran to join the other cows.

Sam remounted Ace. She sat watching as dusk, and then darkness, fell. Sometimes she let her eyes wander to the Calico Mountains.

Over the river and up a rugged trail, the Phantom and his herd were safe.

Here on the range, bumping shoulders and grazing on tender green grass, Buddy was a dark silhouette among others of her kind.

"Everybody's where they belong except us, pretty boy," Sam said, giving her horse a pat.

Lifting her reins, Sam said a silent good-bye to the Phantom, to Buddy, and to the silver moon bouncing on the rippling La Charla River. Then she turned Ace into the summer night and rode at a jog toward home.

From
Phantom Stallion
∾ 12 ∾
RAIN DANCE

More restless than pained, Sunny kept moving around, trying to stay comfortable as the foal positioned itself for birth.

All at once, Blaze bounced to his feet. In the same instant, Sam felt the hair on her arms lift as if she'd taken off a staticky sweater. Then, the air turned blue, the barn shuddered, and—*boom*!

Sam's ears ached as if she'd been thrust to the bottom of a swimming pool.

Sunny's eyes rolled white. She braced her legs and neighed. Outside, the saddle horses answered with frightened calls.

Sam swallowed the scream in her own throat.

Get a grip, she told herself. It was a lightning strike and thunderclap. Close. That's all.

Once the sounds had rolled into silence, Sunny's fear appeared to vanish. Her attention turned inward again. She had her foal to think about.

But what had caused that blue flash? Lightning hitting the house? The bunkhouse? A cottonwood tree that would flare into flame and set everything else on fire?

Sam peered cautiously from the barn doorway and Blaze leaned against her legs. Sparks gnawed along the power lines, bright as Fourth of July fireworks. But not for long. As she watched, the electrical fire sputtered, then disappeared, extinguished by the rain.

"It's okay," she told Blaze. "The power's already out and now the fire is, too."

Sam had only taken a couple of steps away from the barn door when another thought popped into her mind. What if that wasn't a power pole?

She stared at it again. How could she tell the difference between a power pole and a telephone pole?

It didn't matter, she told herself. She either had telephone service or she didn't. Running to the house to check would make no difference.

None.

But she had to know.

Sunny was flicking her tail and stamping her hind hooves as if she wanted to kick.

"I'll be right back, Sunny," Sam promised. "I won't stop for anything. I'll pick up the telephone, listen, and hang up. I promise."

The mare didn't care. Her eyes were wide but her attention was turned inward.

Sam ran. She splashed through the puddles. She felt exposed, as if a lightning bolt were aimed right between her shoulder blades.

I'm halfway safe, she thought as she clattered up the front porch steps and into the kitchen. Crossing every finger, she closed her eyes and lifted the receiver.

Nothing.

She replaced the receiver and lifted it again. Still no dial tone. It *had* been a telephone pole. There was no way to summon help.

Run. Responsibility crashed down on her, and each drop of rain told her to hurry. Dark Sunshine had no one to count on now except for her.

Sam burst back into the barn and pushed her dripping hair away from her face to see Sunny lying on her side, legs straight and stiff. Contractions rippled over her belly.

"I'm here, girl," she whispered to the mare. "That may not sound like much, but I know everything books and cowboys can teach me, and I love you."

As if in response, Sunny half stood. Her front legs trembled with effort and she gave Sam a beseeching stare.

Then, with a slither and a thud, enclosed in a silvery cover, the foal was born.

A celebration started in Sam's head, but she pushed it aside, being sensible.

Clear the membrane from the foal's nose, eyes, and mouth. That's what the book had said. Sam pulled on rubber gloves, but before she could do anything else, a flurry of sound came from the stall.

She could sort of see through the translucent covering.

Legs thrashed and a little head flung from side to

side. Sunny looked back in amazement as slender, black legs kicked and a tiny, slick body bucked on its side.

Ten minutes. The books said the foal might try to stand in ten minutes. This time, the books were wrong.

Free of the silver covering, the storm-born filly struggled to stand.

Now Sam could see her whole body. She had a tiny dished face and huge, luminous eyes. She was satiny black without a speck of white.

Sam realized one of her rubber-gloved hands was pressed against her chest, but her heart had already gone out to the filly.

She'd never seen anything so wonderful. So beautiful.

Only once, her memory chided.

And then Sam remembered.

The tiny black filly looked just like her father.

With a whinny that came out as a squeak, the foal tried to wobble to her feet but failed.

Sunny blinked at the commotion and stared at the foal beside her. The buckskin gave a low nicker. She looked at Sam, then stared into the corner of her stall.

Sam pressed her lips closed. She'd heard herself breathing hard, as if she'd been running.

Don't panic, she told herself. The books said many mares, especially first-time mothers, felt disoriented following their foal's birth.

Poor Sunny. Just minutes ago she'd been alone in her stall. Now a shiny black stranger kicked out at all angles and made little fussing noises.

When Sunny glanced at her again, Sam decided to disappear.

Mother and foal needed time to bond.

In the wild, Sunny would have gone away from the herd. Together, she and her foal would have learned everything about each other. Forever after, Sunny would have known the scent and shape of the foal she had to protect and the foal would know which mare to count on for food and protection.

Sam squatted next to the stall wall and peered through a narrow gap between two boards.

Exhausted from her struggle to stand, the filly trembled. She looked fragile and defenseless.

Rain hammered the roof. Outside, Sam could see raindrops pelting the ground.

The foal was safe and warm in the barn beside her mother, but how would she have survived outside?

The storm's moisture made the pine boards smell like Christmas as Sam stared into the stall to see Sunny sniff her foal's front hooves, then lick her pasterns, then lick as far as her neck would reach, up to the foal's knobby black knees.

The filly was so lightweight, she moved with the force of her mother's tongue, but she seemed to love the attention. When Sunny scooted closer, head extended, the filly mirrored her movements.

Sunny's golden nose was shaded with black around her nostrils and lips. When she touched her baby's muzzle, neither recoiled in surprise. In the lantern light, it was hard to see where one left off and the other began.

That's how it should be, Sam thought, then wished the thought hadn't crossed her mind. Would she ever stop missing her own mother? She wanted to stop wishing she could say, "Hey Mom, look."

Sunny lowered her head and lipped the filly's front legs, then licked them again. Her head bobbed as she did, then her eyelids drooped, her head nodded, and she slept.

Sam watched the foal survey her surroundings. Her tiny black head was about the size of Sam's fisted hands placed end to end. Her eyelids drooped, but instead of sleeping, the foal's head wobbled down, letting her lips touch the straw. Then her head tilted back, barely supported by her weak neck, to look at the rafters.

Take a nap, Sam told her silently, but the filly didn't. Like her father, she was on the alert.

Wind lashed whips of rain through the barn door. Despite the shelter of her stall, the birth-damp filly shivered.

"Time for a rubdown," Sam whispered.

She unfolded the white towel from her foal kit, careful not to allow a molecule of dirt to touch it.

Dr. Scott had said that after mare and baby had

bonded, it was safe to go in and rub the foal dry—if the mare allowed it.

Straightening her knees so slowly she felt like an old woman, Sam stood and looked at Dark Sunshine. The mare's eyes stayed closed.

The foal shivered again and pulled her gangly legs a little closer to her body. If she were too cold, she might stay down, curled up for warmth, instead of standing to nurse. Drying her wet coat would be a good idea.

Sam picked up the bran mash and slid back the bolt on the stall door. She'd use everything she knew about reading the expressions of horses, because she'd seen Sunny with ears pinned back and hatred in her eyes. Tired or not, the mare could wield her teeth and hooves with deadly accuracy.

Sam opened the stall door and slipped inside. She set the bran mash just in front of Sunny. The mare opened her eyes. Though her nostrils quivered at the hearty cereal aroma, she was more interested in Sam.

With weary exasperation, Sunny's expression seemed to ask, "Don't you think I knew you were hiding out there?"

Sam didn't answer, just moved carefully around the edge of the stall.

Never get between a mare and her foal, Dad had told her.

Sam didn't. She kept the foal between them. Even then, Sunny's ears flicked backward. They weren't pinned and her eyes weren't narrowed. Yet.

"You're a good mom, aren't you, Sunny," she crooned to the mare.

The buckskin lay just ahead of the foal nestled at her flank. If the mare stood or made a stronger threat, Sam was determined to run for it.

Rubbing the foal dry was optional, and Sam knew no one would come to her aid if she was injured.

"I promise not to hurt your baby," she said, lowering to her knees, still watching the mare. "You trust me, don't you, girl? I've got to look down to touch her. So, if I do anything you don't like, warn me *before* I get trampled, okay?"

Sam dabbed the soft terry cloth at the foal's eyes and nostrils until they were clean.

The black filly didn't struggle and Sunny didn't protest. After one quiet minute, Sam released the breath she'd been holding. Some books said gentle contact with a foal during its first hour of life could make it friendlier to humans its whole life long.

"And that means you need to stay with me," Sam whispered as she caressed one satiny ear. "Because if you decide to go hang out with your dad, you'll discover not all people are kind."

As she rubbed the filly's inky neck, Sam wondered whether the Phantom had come this afternoon not to steal Dark Sunshine but because he knew his foal was about to be born.

This was no time for wondering. She had to focus

on Sunny and this tiny horse. No matter how gently she massaged, the foal's little head wobbled. The filly was so delicate.

As Sam stroked her short, smooth back, the foal watched with curiosity, but when Sam touched her flank, instinct reminded the filly she was a mustang.

Twig-thin forelegs stiffened, her head ducked in protest, and she let out a high-pitched squeal that made Sam's ears ring.

Eyes clamped on Sunny, Sam scooted away from the filly. One knee back, then the other, then the first one, until her boot sole hit the side of the stall. Slowly, Sam stood.

Sunny's black-rimmed ears tipped forward. Way forward.

Sam knew she should escape while the mare was still trying to puzzle things out.

Quality time with her new horse could wait.

Read the Phantom Stallion books!

AVON BOOKS
An Imprint of HarperCollins*Publishers*
www.harperchildrens.com